Dear Chris

Letters on the Life of Faith

Dear Chris

Letters on the Life of Faith

Warren McWilliams

Baylor University Press
Waco, Texas

Library of Congress Cataloging-in-Publication Data

McWilliams, Warren, 1946-
    Dear Chris : letters on the life of faith / Warren McWilliams.
       p.   cm.
    Includes bibliographical references.
    ISBN 0-918954-70-3 (alk. paper)
    1. Christian life--Baptist authors. I. Title.
BV4515.2.M39   1999
248.4'861--dc21   98-31369
                                          CIP

Cover art by Angela Stanton

Printed in the United States of America on acid-free paper.

DEDICATED TO MY STUDENTS

PAST, PRESENT, AND FUTURE

You yourselves are our letter, written on our hearts, known and read by everybody.

2 Corinthians 3:3 NIV

Contents

Preface

By writing this book I am inviting you to do something most of us consider immoral and illegal, reading another person's mail. The correspondence between Chris and Dr. Mac, however, is fiction, and you are encouraged to read their exchange of letters. I hope that these letters are "true" in the sense of being authentic statements about the Christian life even though they are in a fictional form. They deal with several significant theological and ethical truths related to the Christian life.

Someone once described the apostle Paul's letters as theology in street clothes.[1] I hope that delightful word picture accurately fits the letters presented here as well. This correspondence is designed to help Christians understand some of the basic convictions of their faith more clearly. Like many of the New Testament letters, these reflect real life situations and concerns. Many of the fine points of academic theology are ignored in order that the relevance of the Christian faith for ordinary life might be obvious to the reader. These letters are not intended to be the final word on any subject. Rather, I trust that reading them might prompt some serious reflection on the life of faith. Many of the topics of systematic theology appear in these pages, but I hope that the letter form will help the reader engage these issues in a non-threatening, practical manner.

Although many of my students call me "Dr. Mac," these letters are fiction. Chris is a composite of several of my former students. The questions he raises in our correspondence are typical of the types of questions I am often asked inside and outside of my classrooms. The letters from Dr. Mac in this book generally reflect my thinking on the issues discussed, but occasionally, for the sake of developing the overall story line, I have worded my letters differently than I would in "real life."

I dedicate this book to my students. They consistently challenge and encourage me. Much like Chris, I once struggled with the proper form for my ministry, but over the years my students' response to my teaching has confirmed for me that teaching is the type of ministry for which God prepared me. C. S. Lewis was once described as an ordinary Christian trying to think clearly.[2] I hope the same might be true of me and my students. Together we engage in the study of theology, aptly termed by many Christians "faith seeking understanding."[3]

Although a collection of letters might not seem to have a thesis, the underlying assumption of this correspondence is that each of us needs to develop an authentic, personalized version of the Christian faith. Ideally, these letters will assist the reader in the pilgrimage toward the mature faith that we all seek. Chris's questions are typical of the concerns of many Christians today. These questions are difficult, and the answers are often hard to formulate adequately.

My thanks to David Holcomb of Baylor University Press, who helped this project on the way to publication. I also thank the two anonymous reviewers who read an earlier draft of my work. Their thoughtful comments helped me strengthen my manuscript.

None of my writing would be possible except for the ongoing stimulation and encouragement provided by my family. Patty, Amy, and Karen are theologians in the best sense of the word, for they strive to incarnate the love of God in their daily living. Their "God-talk" is the natural expression of their faith, not the technical jargon that fills my lectures and discussions. University Baptist Church nurtures me by being a community of faith that values both diversity and discipleship. My colleagues at Oklahoma Baptist University continue to amaze me with their enthusiasm for the dialogue between faith and learning. I believe I am a better teacher, a better theologian, and a better Christian as a result of spending most of my professional career in their midst.

Warren McWilliams

P. S. Except for this preface, all documentation is provided at the end of the book. "Endnotes" are not natural to correspondence, but Dr. Mac and Chris occasionally mention sources and quotations that you might want to pursue.

Notes

1.   Richard Melick, *Philippians, Colossians, Philemon* (Nashville, TN: Broadman, 1991), 46.

2.   Peter Kreeft, *Between Heaven and Hell* (Downers Grove, IL: InterVarsity, 1982), 25.

3.   For a recent interpretation of this classic description of the nature and task of theology, see Daniel L. Migliore, *Faith Seeking Understanding: An Introduction to Christian Theology* (Grand Rapids, MI: Eerdmans, 1991), 2-5.

Dear Chris

Letters on the Life of Faith

1

What Are the Questions?

November 15

Dear Dr. Mac,

Seeing you at Homecoming last weekend was a pleasant surprise. I'm glad you got to meet Carolyn and our kids. Although I've only been gone from college for 5 years, a lot has happened to me. Since we just got to chat for a few minutes at the half time of the basketball game, I thought I would update you a little more on what's happened to me since graduation.

The last time I saw you I was headed to seminary. (By the way, I don't know if I ever thanked you for the letter of recommendation. So, Thanks!) I had been having a few reservations about my call to the ministry during my senior year, and I thought going to a non-Baptist seminary might let me think through my beliefs and my vocation. I remember that you took one of your degrees at a non-Baptist school as well. Anyway, I started to seminary eager to clarify my call to the ministry and to solidify my beliefs.

I finished one year of seminary, but then I dropped out of school. I met Carolyn at the church I joined that year, we fell in love, and we got married after that first year of seminary. I guess I used the marriage and my new family responsibilities as an excuse, but I didn't go back to school that fall. I found a job as a reporter for the local newspaper; I suppose the English minor finally helped! Well, after four years of marriage and two kids, we decided to come back for Homecoming. I wanted Carolyn to meet some of my college friends and profs.

I have to admit I was a little embarrassed to see you last weekend. After 5 years I figured I would have worked through my theological quandaries, got my seminary degree, and be on a church staff, preferably in Texas! Well, I haven't pursued my theological education, and I know you were always a stickler for ministerial students getting as much education as possible. Also, my job at the newspaper isn't very "religious" or ministerial. We're able to pay our bills, but I sometimes wonder if I should have stayed in seminary and taken a church position. At any rate, I wanted you to know that I really appreciated you as a teacher. Maybe it won't be 5 years before I get back again.

> Sincerely,
> Chris

November 21

Dear Chris,

Thanks for your letter. I really did enjoy our brief chat at the basketball game, and your letter filled in some details. I had lost track of you, but Homecoming is always a good time to catch up.

Meeting the rest of your family was a real pleasure, but I could tell you were a little uneasy. Your letter helped me see what was on your mind. You're right, I do stress the need for education for ministers. Some of my students probably think it's a party line, since I am a teacher. Unfortunately, I don't always make it clear enough that education can be gained in a lot of ways. For example, when I was in college I learned as much outside of the classroom as in it. Conversations in the cafeteria or bull sessions in the dorm can be very informative! Also, some very fine ministers have limited formal training. They have worked hard at self-education. Ideally, learning is a lifelong activity. A few weeks ago a former student left a note on my office door. He signed it, "A former student, still learning." I like that!

Although I realize that Christians should be concerned about the total person, as an educator I really stress loving God with our minds. When Jesus was asked about the great commandment, he quoted from the Old Testament. He mentioned that we should love God with our minds, an idea not included in the OT version. (Compare Matt. 22:37 with Deut. 6:5). Even if you never do any more "formal" education, with classrooms and teachers, I hope you will continue to study and think about the Christian faith. You probably remember that I consider all Christians to be "theologians" because we all think about God. I like Martin Luther's description of a theologian: A "person becomes a theologian by living, by dying and by being damned, not by understanding, reading and speculating." (Excuse the "earthy" language!) Book-learning, as the old-timers call it, has its place, but I'm sure you have learned a lot about life and the Christian faith since you left seminary.

You also mentioned that your newspaper job was not especially "religious." Here you've opened one of those proverbial cans of worms! Our Baptist tradition has put us in an interesting dilemma. On one hand, we argue strongly for the priesthood of believers. We are suspicious of denominations that keep a sharp boundary between clergy and laity. We believe that all Christians are priests or ministers. The denomination that supports the seminary you attended, for instance, also has a strong emphasis on the priesthood of all believers. Like Baptists, they still ordain clergy. On the other hand, Baptists have fought some of our biggest battles over the nature of the ministry. In particular, we're still debating about ordination. Like another prof said, the two biggest influences on our view of ordination are the Internal Revenue Service and the Roman Catholic Church! Even though Protestants talk a lot about all Christians being priests, there is still a pecking order: foreign missionaries, home missionaries, pastors, and so on have a higher call, some believe, than ordinary lay people.

Without boring you with my views on ordination, let me add that you shouldn't worry that you have "left the ministry." Although I do believe that God calls some people into vocational Christian ministry, most Christians are ministers through "secular" careers as well as their church and family activities. Perhaps, if we talked some more, we could begin to sort out your understanding of your call. When you were a student here I know you spoke of an experience of being called to the ministry. Perhaps you interpreted some dramatic spiritual experience as a call. Sometimes young people interpret a very vivid encounter with God as a "call" when it is actually not. Or, perhaps God is still preparing you for your ministry. Certainly many of the great leaders of the Bible had significant life experiences before they entered the ministry! Or, maybe your job as a reporter is your "ministry." In some church history class you probably heard about Martin Luther's idea that any occupation can be a vocation ("calling") if we honor God through it.

Well, I'm not really a very good correspondent (I tend to ramble), but I wanted you to know that I was glad to get your letter. Keep in touch.

Sincerely,
Dr. Mac

P. S. I recently got an e-mail system for my computer at school. If you want to correspond that way, I think I've figured out how to use the technology! My address is on my business card I'm enclosing.

From: Chris
To: Dr. Mac
Date: December 2
Subject: Questions

It's taken me a few days to get up the courage to write you again. I was afraid you would be very disappointed in what I was doing now, but your letter was surprisingly supportive. Oh, I didn't mean to sound as if I thought you wouldn't understand. Although you have a well-deserved reputation as a hard teacher, I know you really care about your students. Anyway, thanks for your letter.

While I'm being honest, I need to add one more confession. I mentioned to you that I had dropped out of seminary for family reasons. That is only partly true. For the last couple of years Carolyn and I have not been very active in the church. Our family life has been kind of hectic (2 kids in 4 years), but that's not the real reason. Actually, I've had some real questions about the institutional church and what it's teaching. These questions surfaced late in my college career, and my year of seminary did not erase my concerns. Carolyn and I talked about this while we dated, and she, too, had some theological concerns.

I suppose the church we attended here was OK, but I felt increasingly out of step with most of the membership. I don't mean I have lost my faith in God or anything nearly that radical, but I feel a real uneasiness with where the church is. My work as a reporter has really opened my eyes about the so-called real world. I never felt college was a spiritual ghetto or hot-house, but I was still pretty naive about life and faith when I graduated. Now I'm not so sure what I believe.

I know you said you're not a very good correspondent, but I wonder if you would be willing to keep on writing to me. That is, if I can formulate my concerns into a few coherent questions. I know you used to tell us in theology class that your main job was not to create clones of you, but I would like to bounce a few ideas off you occasionally. Let me know what you think. I am impressed that you're using e-mail these days.

From: Dr. Mac
To: Chris
Date: December 15
Subject: Questions—Reply

You're on! I'd be glad to write to you, if you think it would help you with your questions. I'm sure it would help me to try to clarify some ideas in short messages. Besides, you've already heard the long, windy lectures.

Your last e-mail reminded me of the opening line of one of my favorite theology books: "Human life is a dialogue between expectation and experience." Although thinking about our faith can be pretty boring (I'm thinking of theology textbooks, not any theology teachers you or I know), your recent experiences have alerted you to some important issues.

I sense that you're not quite sure where to begin. Somehow most education does a better job at giving us "answers" than helping us formulate the questions. I still like Tom Skinner's book title, *If Christ Is the Answer, What Are the Questions?* Or, maybe you've seen the TV commercials that use the slogan, "Real Life, Real Answers." After describing a family financial predicament, the financial consultants recommend a solution. One profitable way to look at theology is as a dialogue between the questions of real life and the theological answers rooted in scripture.

Some of my current students seem to already have all of the answers. I hope I can help them see what questions really matter. A few years ago I went to England on a brief study tour. I like the description of theology in Oxford University's catalogue. "To enjoy Theology you need above all to be interested in the questions it raises, and not too sure about all the answers." I'm convinced the Christian faith has the basic answers to life's questions, but unfortunately we don't listen to the questions too well. Theologians and other Christians often offer pat answers to tough questions.

Since we're in the Advent season now, I'm not sure how consistent our correspondence will be. My only e-mail is here in my office. I do come in during the holidays, but I'll probably catch up on most of my correspondence after Christmas. If you have time over the holidays, you might see if you still have the "confession of faith" you wrote for our theology class. Remember, for that assignment you summarized your personal theology. If you read it over, you might know where to start. I would be willing to tackle any of the doctrines, but you let me know what is most puzzling or interesting to you now. I'm used to being a sounding board for my students, and I often learn a lot from those exchanges. Merry Christmas!

2

Why Jesus?

From: Chris
To: Dr. Mac
Date: December 26
Subject: Jesus

I appreciate your willingness to keep up our correspondence. I'm sure it would be easier to pick up the telephone,
but that would be expensive! When I took English courses
in college, I discovered I could think better when I wrote out
my ideas. Writing these "letters" to you may help me clarify
my questions, and using e-mail eliminates most of the expense. Besides, I remember you were sometimes hard to
catch in your office for a phone call. You used to like to
engage in "interdisciplinary dialogues with colleagues," or
what the rest of us called coffee breaks! I know you may
not see this message until after the holidays, but today has
been a slow news day at work.

I've decided that the issue we ought to start with is Jesus. I
mentioned in my last letter that Carolyn and I have sort of

dropped out of church in the last few years, but we attended a Christmas Eve service at our church this week. Maybe it was just a nostalgia trip, or perhaps we felt guilty that our kids were seeing only the secular side of Christmas on TV and in the mall. Singing the Christmas carols and seeing the little kids do the traditional Christmas story, with bathrobes and crooked coat hanger halos, started me thinking again about Jesus.

The pastor's devotional was called "The Reason for the Season." I've seen that slogan a lot lately; I guess it's the "in" response to the commercialization of Christmas that church leaders have protested for years. Still, the devotional touched a sensitive spot in my thinking. I followed up on your last suggestion and dug out my "confession of faith" from your class on "Christian Doctrines." I wasn't surprised that I kept it. I'm really a pack rat, and I remember how I sweated over putting my theology on paper.

When I read what I had written 5 years ago about all of the major doctrines, I was astounded at how traditional I sounded. I know I came to college with a very old-fashioned set of beliefs. Although I had some doubts and questions through the four years of college, I suppose I really didn't get serious about my faith until I left. Any serious questions I had at college I tried to keep to myself, and I apparently did not include them in my "confession of faith." I guess that "confession" was not as honest as it should have been. I probably worried then that expressing doubts would cause friends and even professors to think I was a weak Christian. Now that I've lived outside of the safe confines of a Christian college and church for a few years, I think I can be more open about my theological questions.

So, let's start with Jesus. In particular, why do Christians believe he is unique or special? In my work as a reporter I meet all kinds of people. Many of them are not religious at all, and some follow other religions. Although I still live in the "Bible belt," it's amazing how pluralistic this town is. In addition to many Christian denominations, several other religions have meetings here. If these other groups claim to have an inside track with God, how can Christians justify their belief in Jesus as the one true way to God? Why is Jesus more special than Moses, Buddha, or Mohammed?

I realize you're on Christmas break now, but I look forward to hearing from you soon.

From: Dr. Mac
To: Chris
Date: January 6
Subject: Jesus—Reply

I found your e-mail when I got back on campus after Christmas. Classes started today for our January term. As usual, I'm teaching "Biblical Ethics." For someone like me, trained primarily in theology, it's a real stretch to be competent in another area, but I really like teaching the subject *and* the students. Unfortunately, I'll have a lot of term papers to read at the end of the month.

Starting with Jesus is fine. In fact, I can't think of any better place. One textbook in systematic theology (by Morris Ashcraft) started with Jesus as the first major topic. Our textbook from 5 years ago started with the topic of revelation. (Of course, he spent some time on "prolegomena" before he tackled any major doctrines. Those "preliminary remarks" took about 100 pages as I recall. No one in your class seemed to revel in the fine points of subjects such as the definitions, assumptions, and methods of theology!)

Of course, as I pointed out many, many times one characteristic of systematic theology is that all doctrines are somehow intertwined. If I ever get around to writing a systematic theology textbook, I'll have to wrestle with the issue of sequence. Since I'll be trying to help you sort out some issues, I'll let you set the agenda.

Why do Christians believe Jesus is unique? You certainly chose a tough issue to get us started! There are a lot of ways to get a handle on this issue. Let me mention a couple of approaches, and you let me know which one you want to pursue. First, discussing the uniqueness of Jesus presupposes our understanding of God's revelation of himself to us. I'm willing to start with the presupposition that God would want to reveal himself to us. Hypothetically a creator God might not want the creatures to know about him, but I will assume that a good, loving God would want to reveal something of his character to his creatures. To defend that view would take us into the fields of philosophy of religion and Christian apologetics before we went deeper into the topic of Christology.

By the way, I struggle with the pronouns for God. The gender of God issue is complex, and thoughtful Christians realize God is beyond gender. I'll use the traditional masculine pronouns, but I don't mean God is male. Maybe we'll tackle this issue later on.

Back to the subject of revelation. God has revealed himself in various ways: historical events, miracles, visions, angels, and the beauty of nature. One of my favorites is the Urim and Thummim, the sacred dice used by the priests in the Old Testament to determine God's will (for example, Exodus 28:30).

You recall that theologians usually distinguish two major types of revelation, general revelation and special revelation. General revelation is God's disclosure of himself to everyone through the created world, human nature, and human history. Special revelation is God's revelation to specific people at specific times, such as the revelation recorded in the Bible. The revelation in Jesus is traditionally taken by Christians to be the supreme, fullest revelation of God in human history.

In our class I mentioned that Christians have held a variety of views across the centuries on the value or validity of general revelation. What can we know about God apart from special revelation, especially the Bible? Some Christians have argued that we can develop a valid "natural theology" based on general revelation. In other words, you can know quite a bit about God without looking at the Bible (such as he exists, he is powerful, he is good, he is holy). You might recall a typology I drew on the blackboard in class. I've enclosed a version of it as a graphic file (I hope your software can accommodate this).

Enclosure:

A	B	C
GR Yes	GR Yes	GR No
NT Yes	NT No	NT No
SR Yes	SR Yes	SR Yes

| | ─────────────── | | ─────────────── | | |

GR=general revel.   NT=natural theology   SR=special revel.

Theologians in group A see the most value to general revelation. Because they emphasize general revelation and natural theology, they sometimes seem a little fuzzy on the uniqueness of Jesus. People in group B oppose natural theology because sin has clouded our ability to see God in the world around us. Still, they agree that the revelation is objectively there. A tree (revelation) has fallen in the forest, but we are too deaf (to change from a visual to an auditory illustration) to hear the revelation. The group that is the strongest on special revelation is group C. They even deny that there is any general revelation, so, obviously, there can be no natural theology built on it.

Well, without redoing an entire week of theology lectures, you see that we might want to look at the uniqueness of Jesus in light of the debate about general and special revelation.

A second approach would be to limit our attention to what the Bible says about Jesus. I don't mean that we have to agree on the uniqueness of Jesus before we talk about it! That wouldn't be fair. Rather, I mean that we could follow a courtroom analogy and admit the testimony about Jesus. The verdict about the testimony will be open until we discuss the issue some more. If you saw the old "Oh, God" movies (weren't there 2?), you recall that God got to defend himself before a group of church leaders and theologians! Personally, I thought Santa Claus did a better job in the movie "Miracle on 34th Street" (not the one where color was added, please).

One of my favorite theologians, C. S. Lewis, focused his discussion on Jesus' claims about himself. Lewis insisted that, in light of what Jesus said about who he was, we could not call him merely a great teacher. "He would either be a lunatic—on the level with the man who says he is a poached egg—or else he would be the Devil of Hell. Either this man was, and is, the Son of God: or else a madman or something worse." This version of the issue has been popularized as the Lord/Liar/Lunatic dilemma (or trilemma). At any rate, it argues that Jesus leaves us with a forced option about his uniqueness.

Well, I've written a lot and haven't really scratched the surface of your question. Let me know if either approach sounds more profitable to you. I need to review some notes for class tomorrow. By the way, today is Epiphany, the traditional date for the visit of the wise men to the baby Jesus. (January 6 is also my oldest daughter's birthday.) I'll pray that we find some wisdom for our correspondence about Jesus.

From: Chris
To: Dr. Mac
Date: January 12
Subject: Lord/Liar/Lunatic

I had to read your e-mail several times. To be honest, I had forgotten that my simple question could be so complex. I guess I had hoped that you could pronounce some magical formula and all of my questions (doubts?) would disappear. I found both of your angles or approaches intriguing. If I had some ongoing contact with someone from another religion, I'm sure I would want to pursue the general revelation angle. I guess my question about the uniqueness of Jesus could be another form of the old issue, "What about the heathen who have never heard about Jesus?" Although that issue is *very* interesting to me, I'm afraid it's more a matter of intellectual curiosity than a real life issue for me right now. So, let's put that version of the issue on the back burner for awhile. Your brief comment on the gender of God was intriguing, but maybe I'll get back to it later!

Your second approach sounded vaguely familiar. I know the Lord/Liar/Lunatic formula rang a bell. My reaction to that formula has usually been that it was a little too neat and clever. Maybe I'm also rebelling against all of those sermons that used 3 points that alliterate! Any way, I'm willing to try it out. My serious objection to the formula would be that it really doesn't prove that Jesus is the Son of God or unique. Logically it only states a forced option. Why couldn't a skeptic (and I don't mean that I am one!) simply opt for the liar or lunatic. I recall that "M*A*S*H" was your favorite TV show. On one episode a character claimed he was Jesus Christ, but everyone knew that he needed psychological help.

Well, I think that's the direction I would like to go for now. I conducted several interviews this morning, and I need to meet a deadline at the newspaper.

From: Dr. Mac
To: Chris
Date: January 20
Subject: Lord/Liar/Lunatic—Reply

Before I begin grading a set of tests, I'll try to get us a few steps farther down the road. I hope I didn't leave the wrong impression by using a 3 point, alliterative outline. Certainly neither the C. S. Lewis quotation nor the Lord/Liar/Lunatic formula proves that Jesus is unique. But they do remind us that there are limited options once we agree that Jesus claimed to be unique. I know you stay very busy, but occasionally I might want to recommend a book you might want to read. If you have already looked at Lewis's *Mere Christianity,* you might enjoy how some of his ideas are developed in Peter Kreeft's *Beyond Heaven and Hell.* I've learned a lot from several of Kreeft's books. Like most teachers, I'm trained to give my sources; I wouldn't want to be guilty of plagiarism. In Kreeft's book, Lewis debates with John Kennedy and Aldous Huxley about several theological issues. (Oh, the trivia here is that all three of these men died on the same day, Nov. 22, 1963).

Kreeft argues that the issue of what we think of Jesus is the biggest one in Christian apologetics. Although apologetics is typically an intellectual defense of the faith before skeptics, I find a lot of Christians, like you and me, at times have questions about their faith. If we grant that Jesus claimed to be divine, then he is divine or is a bad man (morally or psychologically). One objection to this scheme is that Jesus never really claimed to be unique; stated bluntly, some scholars argue that the New Testament material is legendary. Lewis defends the authenticity of the New Testament. If you want to discuss that issue, let me know. The notoriety of the Jesus Seminar in recent years has brought these issues into the news magazines. So far, however, I don't detect that the big issues about the Bible (such as its inspiration, interpretation, or inerrancy) are at the heart of your concern.

Another objection to the Lord/Liar/Lunatic scheme is that all people are divine, so Jesus' claim to divinity is not unique at all. Pantheists, for instance, assume a basic identity between God and all of reality. ("All = God" was my classroom formula for pantheism). Pantheism has been prevalent in many religions and philosophies and is one of the primary beliefs of New Age thinking. A Christian view of God as creator and us as creatures rules out a pantheistic or total identification of the infinite and finite. If you want to pursue this issue, we could evaluate several of the major world views that are alternatives to Christianity.

At any rate, I think Lewis is correct that we have only a limited number of alternatives about Jesus, in light of what Jesus said about himself. He doesn't prove Jesus is divine, but he forces a decision.

Let me know where you want to go next. Right now, I'd better devote some of my brain power to grading those tests. When those papers are done, I'll face final exams!

From: Chris
To: Dr. Mac
Date: January 31
Subject: Incarnation

I appreciate your willingness to write to me about my theological questions. Maybe I'll have to give something to the
phonathon this year! I suppose the college still has profs
and others calling alums for donations. I have such a strong
dislike for phone solicitors that I haven't given to the
phonathon yet. Maybe this year I'll make a small pledge.

You sounded so enthusiastic about the Kreeft book that I
took your advice and found a copy in a local used book
store. I just started reading it, and it may help me. I won't
send you a full-fledged book review, but I'll let you know
what I think later.

Right now I think I have a new twist on my original question. If I assume that Jesus was (is?) God in human form,
how do I explain how that happened? I remember from our
theology class that "incarnation," the traditional term, is not
even a biblical term (did you say it was based on Latin?). I
don't want you to think that I stay awake at night thinking
up these strange questions, but our correspondence has
really got me to thinking about theology again. I know you
warned us against tying ourselves into theological pretzels,
but I'm confused!

What triggered this confusion was a discussion Carolyn and
I had after a TV program recently. She's been reading our
exchanges (I hope you don't mind) and asked me how God
becoming one of us in Jesus of Nazareth differed from the
experiences of Sam Beckett on "Quantum Leap." I watched
this series a little when I was in college, and we've seen it

in syndication lately. I used to think that college profs, especially religion profs, never watched TV, but your examples from "M*A*S*H" shot that theory down. Anyway, Beckett "leaps" (through some kind of time travel) into a different person in each episode in order to change history for the better. I realized I didn't know enough to answer Carolyn's question intelligently. Maybe you'll have time during the spring semester to continue our discussion. If not, let me know.

From: Dr. Mac
To: Chris
Date: February 5
Subject: Incarnation—Reply

Thank goodness you realize that professors watch TV! In fact, I now insist that watching TV is part of my "research." Maybe you recall that I've dabbled in theology of popular culture (TV, movies, comic strips). Robert Short's books on the Peanuts comic strip really got me interested in how our basic values as Americans are reflected in popular media. Of course, I still read industrial-strength theologians such as Barth, Moltmann, McFague, and Calvin, but I find I can strike a responsive chord with a lay audience a lot faster with an example from a comic strip rather than a quotation from an academic theologian.

But, to get back to Carolyn's question about the difference between Sam Beckett's leaping and Jesus' incarnation: I don't know! I've watched "Quantum Leap" several times, and I even asked my theology students last semester if they thought an orthodox Christology could be developed with that model. As you might expect, we did not reach a clear consensus.

I still teach that the "orthodox" view of Jesus, held by all major denominations, is captured in the early creeds of the church. Trying to state orthodox belief in contemporary terms, however, is a real challenge. As a minimum, Christians want to say that Jesus is truly divine and truly human. The debates in early Christian history were partly a struggle to set clear boundaries between heresy and orthodoxy.

My hunch is that a "Quantum Leap" Christology would be too close to Apollinarianism to be orthodox. Since I don't assume that you remember all of the names for those ancient heresies, I'll give an oversimplified definition. Apollinarius argued that Jesus had a human body and a divine soul or spirit. The early church considered that a heresy because they affirmed that Jesus had a complete human personality in addition to the presence of God. When Sam Beckett leaps into someone else's body, the other personality disappears for awhile. (Has the show ever explained that?) Orthodox Christians insisted that Jesus was fully human, not partially human. He was also fully divine.

I realize that this is all very strange. If Carolyn reads this letter, she will believe every odd thing you've ever told her about theology in general or theologians like me in particular! I am glad you're letting Carolyn read our e-mail.

My wife and I correspond with different people, and we often read each other's letters. As you would guess, we have very few secrets.

From: Chris
To: Dr. Mac
Date: February 8
Subject: Incarnation—Reply—Reply

Carolyn asked me to ask you to follow up on your last e-mail. What do you mean by an "orthodox" view of Jesus? Carolyn thought you might mean a denomination, such as Greek Orthodox or Russian Orthodox, but I couldn't really help her much. I thought a quick e-mail might be simpler than reviewing my theology textbook or my class notes.

From: Dr. Mac
To: Chris
Date: February 9
Subject: Orthodox View of Jesus

Good question from Carolyn. Let me clarify a little without sounding too much like a professional theologian. I'm using "orthodox" in the basic sense of "correct beliefs." The correct beliefs about Jesus would be the consensus view of the early church, a view the church reached through a series of major councils.

I do not believe that contemporary Christians have to memorize and repeat those ancient church creeds and confessions, but I believe those Christians worked hard at declaring their beliefs clearly and at avoiding dangerous views, what we call heresies. We can be guided by the wisdom of the early church even when we express our beliefs in contemporary terms.

Beyond that basic definition of "orthodox," however, I would add a few personal observations. First, I am willing to use the language of paradox to describe Jesus. I think paradoxical language is essential for capturing some of the polarities and tensions I see in the biblical witness about Jesus. To say Jesus is both divine and human is logically contradictory in some logical systems, but the Bible seems to have its own "logic" or distinctive way of determining what "makes sense." A lot of other doctrines are also paradoxical; for example, God is both transcendent and immanent. Many heresies are the result of neglecting or denying one side of a paradoxical biblical truth.

One reason why the incarnation seems so illogical to some people is that they begin with abstract or non-biblical definitions of divine and human. They struggle with trying to glue these two natures together. If we begin with the reality of Jesus, then our understanding of both the divine and the human is controlled or guided by the revelation in Jesus.

Second, the early creeds are valuable for reminding us that there are boundaries in describing Jesus. Although you and I would not want to use all of their technical jargon (remember the debate about *homoousios* and *homoiousious*?), the early church's intent was sound. To say "I believe in Jesus" is fine as a simple testimony, but when alternative views of Jesus exist, we need to clarify which view is most adequate to scripture and our experience. Perhaps the earliest Christian confession was "Jesus is Lord." Those words are simple, but thinking about the implications and consequences of that statement can be staggering.

Third, I am increasingly convinced about the priority of images (word pictures, metaphors, stories) for theology. The biblical writers seem to focus on concrete images more than conceptual, propositional language. Both kinds of language are important, but I do not see the biblical writers worrying so much about working out a precise, theoretical view of Jesus. Christians should not shirk their duty to explain the faith, but too many battles have been fought over theories. I still take "faith seeking understanding" as a valuable description of theology. In fact, our correspondence is really an exercise in that "seeking" of a fuller understanding. I hope I will not bog down in too much theoretical nit-picking.

One theologian suggested that the New Testament used three models to describe the unity of Jesus as God and man. First, the *gnosis* (knowledge) model focuses on Jesus' special, intimate knowledge of God. Matthew 11:25-27 illustrates that approach: Jesus has a special knowledge of God the

Father, and he shares that knowledge with his followers. Second, Paul's famous hymn in Philippians 2:5-11 illustrates the *kenosis* (empty) model. When the Son "emptied" himself, he became one of us (v.7). Entire books have been devoted to the theory of kenoticism, but Paul offers only a metaphor or word picture. Third, the *skenosis* (tent) model is based on John 1:14. Jesus, the Word, became flesh and pitched his tent with us. As one translator put it, "The Word became flesh and blood, and moved into the neighborhood." None of these word pictures is totally satisfactory, but they are pointers to the reality of God's presence in Jesus.

If I were to choose one verse that epitomizes my Christology, it would probably be 2 Corinthians 5:19. "God was in Christ, reconciling the world unto himself...." "God was in Christ" does not answer all of my questions, but it seems to be a simple, basic affirmation for a Christian testimony. Whether God was in Christ in the same way Sam Beckett leaps into a new character each week is not clear. We really are back to your original questions about the uniqueness of Jesus. The Bible points to a unique incarnation of God in Jesus, while Sam Beckett is "incarnate" in someone new each week. Although I want to affirm the uniqueness of Jesus, I do not deny that God has been present in some mysterious, powerful way in many people, such as Moses, Elijah, Deborah, Esther, Peter, and Mary. One of my favorite books took Paul's description as the title, *God Was In Christ* by Donald Baillie. Of course, I don't agree with everything Baillie says, but his book is a solid overview of the issues.

God was in Christ in some special, unique way; Jesus is the Son of God. I can't prove Jesus is God in human form, but I take the New Testament evidence very seriously. For example, the early Christians called Jesus "Lord." Jewish people would have thought of God as Lord. The Jews believed that the name Yahweh, given to Moses at the burning bush, was too sacred to say out loud, so they said "Lord" (Adonai) whenever Yahweh appeared in the text. A Jewish Christian calling Jesus Lord would be saying Jesus is God.

The best evidence for the deity of Jesus is his resurrection. The New Testament records some other types of evidence as well, including Jesus' "I am" sayings (such as John 14:6), his miracles, and his virgin conception and birth.

Well, I may be restating the issue rather than helping you much. At the very least, perhaps I have given you some extra grist for the mill (although I keep forgetting that students don't understand some of my word pictures) or food for thought.

Our second semester has barely begun, but life is hectic again. Let me know what you're thinking.

3

Who Are You, Really?

From: Chris
To: Dr. Mac
Date: February 14
Subject: Gospels

Thanks for a very informative letter. I was glad that you explained your interest in images and metaphors a little. Although I never took your course in "Contemporary Theology," you used to mention your interest in "story theology" as a good corrective to some of the theoretical debates in theology. You asked so much of the technical jargon on your tests, however, that I often had the impression that you thought all Christians ought to talk that way! Maybe if I had had more opportunities to hear you preach and teach in churches I would have realized you could talk in lay terms. As a reporter and news writer, I understand the power of images, both visual and verbal. A picture is worth a 1000 words is true, at least in journalism. A word picture can be much more powerful than a dull, abstract sentence. I had never thought about how important images would be for theology as well.

I wanted you know that our correspondence is helping me and Carolyn. No, we haven't started attending church every service, but we are going more often than before. Also, we've tried to do some Bible study again. Because you stressed the New Testament evidence or testimony about Jesus, we decided to read through the gospels again. Although I do not yet see the need for some of the sophisticated jargon of those early church creeds, I am especially watching for what Jesus has to say about himself.

One of the interesting things I noticed is how often Jesus says why he came. He was pretty clear about his purpose or agenda during his life. Some of my favorites are the following:

"For even the Son of Man did not come to be served, but to serve, and to give his life as a ransom for many." (Mark 10:45)

"For the Son of Man came to seek and to save what was lost." (Luke 19:10)

"I have come that they may have life, and have it to the full." (John 10:10b)

I realize that I will need more than these few verses to develop a view of Christ that is satisfactory to me, but right now they help. I guess one of my real concerns has been that I inherited a set of beliefs that made sense for awhile, but now I need to find a theology that is really mine. I know I won't need to reinvent the wheel, but our correspondence has been the catalyst for me to do some serious thinking about Jesus.

From: Dr. Mac
To: Chris
Date: February 20
Subject: Gospels—Reply

I'm glad you and Carolyn have started doing some Bible study. Our correspondence has been beneficial for me as well. I have tried for years to balance the need for my students to be familiar with the jargon of theology with their need to translate their faith into contemporary terms. Like any academic discipline, theology has its own specialized terms, and I do ask a lot of them on tests. More important than the terms, however, are the ideas and experiences they represent. I hope the next time I teach theology I will be more sensitive to the perception that jargon gets in the way of understanding the issues and preparing my students for ministry.

Your short list of Bible passages about the purpose of Jesus' ministry was very intriguing, and it would be a good way to introduce my Christology unit. I could ask my students "What did Jesus come to do" and have them do the kind of Bible study you've begun. When you have finished that list, I'd like to have a copy; I borrow teaching material from lots of good sources! By the way, you might want to look outside of the gospels. For example, in Hebrews 10:7 Jesus said, "I have come to do your will, O God."

You may recall that theologians have often debated the best place to start in discussing Jesus. Since you initially asked me about the uniqueness of Jesus, our discussion dwelt on Christology, or the doctrine of the person of Christ. This topic usually includes treatment of evidence for his deity (topics such as virgin conception, miracles, witness of the apostles, resurrection), evidence for his humanity (emotions, fatigue, hunger, thirst), and the unity of these 2 "natures." Certainly we have not covered all of those issues, but the discussion of Jesus' uniqueness is one aspect of Christology.

Within the field of Christology, some debate about doing Christology "from above" or "from below." A Christology from above starts with belief in the deity of Jesus and tries to explain how he became one of us. The incarnation is the central intellectual puzzle. A Christology from below tries to follow the thought process of the early disciples, who first encountered Jesus as a very unusual human and later concluded he was also God's Son. I won't try to sort out the details of these two models in our correspondence. They both can be orthodox in their conclusions.

Some theologians insist, however, that discussions of Christology easily become too speculative or theoretical.

For example, when the Son "emptied" himself (Phil. 2:7), what did he give up? Although I like the word picture of *kenosis,* I realize how strange some of those discussions can get. Melanchthon's famous dictum has been accepted by many: "To know Christ is to know his benefits." To these thinkers, soteriology rather Christology is the best starting point for discussions of Jesus. Soteriology is the doctrine of the work of Christ, or the doctrine of the savior.

If you saw the movie "Pale Rider," you might recall that Clint Eastwood is the mysterious preacher who helps some oppressed people. One person eventually asks him, "Who are you, really?" The priority here is on what Jesus has done for us (salvation); then we try to discern his exact identity (Christology). When I was very young, I used to watch the "Lone Ranger" TV series. After the Lone Ranger had settled some problem, someone would ask, "Who was that masked man?"

In our theology class we studied several atonement theories that develop the New Testament evidence on the "work" of Christ. Your study of what Jesus came to do would be important data for that kind of discussion.

I'm afraid I turned into a teacher again and told you more than you wanted to know. This correspondence has been stimulating to me. I hope you are learning as much as I have. I was a little slow getting back to you this time. My younger daughter's birthday was February 16, and we had a family celebration planned.

From: Chris
To: Dr. Mac
Date: March 2
Subject: Atonement

Carolyn wanted me to thank you for sharing your ideas on theology. She was an accounting major at a state university. Although she was active in her church as a youth, she's never dug as deep into the fine points of theology as I have. Your letters have given us a lot to talk about—once we get the kids to bed!

I'm still reading through the gospels, but I'll keep my eyes open for other statements about Jesus' mission as I get into the rest of the New Testament. I guess I'm enjoying my reading of the Bible more because my attention is focused. Sometimes I saw it as a kind of chore to get done each day. In fact, I dug out my Greek lexicon to check on some of the key words. I found that Jesus used the word *zoe* for "life" a lot in John's gospel. But, I suppose you already knew that! Anyway, one of my seminary textbooks said that this Greek word emphasized that Jesus offered us a special quality of life, not just more of the same (*bios,* physical life). Very interesting!

When you mentioned soteriology in your last e-mail, I realized that I had never really figured out exactly what I believe about Jesus' death. When I looked in my "confession of faith" from your class, all I found was one line: "I believe that Jesus died for my sins." I know we discussed several atonement theories in class, but that's all I included in my personal theology. You didn't make many comments on my paper about my meager statement. You did write in the margin, "Do you lean toward any of the major atonement theories?" In a way I see a connection between my initial question about Jesus' uniqueness and the atonement. Why does the death of Jesus matter so much?

If you have time, maybe we can correspond a little about your view of the atonement.

From: Dr. Mac
To: Chris
Date: March 13
Subject: Atonement—Reply

We're getting near spring break here, so I thought I ought to let you know I would be quite willing to continue our correspondence.

I'm not surprised that you had such a brief statement on soteriology or that I made no comments. My question about your favorite atonement theory was designed to see if you leaned towards any of the classic explanations of the significance of Jesus' death. I didn't mean you had to choose one view and reject the others. In fact, there is an element of truth in most atonement theories.

One simple reason for my not pressing you to say more about atonement is that soteriology has never been quite as controversial in church history as Christology. No major councils met to debate the fine points of atonement theory. Most evangelicals would be satisfied with your brief statement since it focuses on the key event, the death of Jesus, and interprets it in a substitutionary way ("died for my sins").

As you would guess by now, I would want to stress the importance of the biblical images for a fuller understanding of atonement. One of my favorite passages to illustrate the richness and variety of the New Testament imagery is Romans 3:24-25. Having just demonstrated the universality of sin, Paul offers three images for salvation. First, Jesus "justified" us. Here Paul used a legal term in a totally non-legalistic way. Although we are guilty as sinners, God has pardoned us. Second, Jesus is our "redemption." This term comes from the practice of slavery. Redemption is essentially liberation from bondage. Third, Jesus is the "sacrifice of atonement." Here the NIV uses a phrase to capture one Greek word, the word for the top of the ark of the covenant (the "mercy seat"). Jesus accomplished for us what the Hebrew sacrificial system tried to do. He is the perfect sacrifice.

The famous atonement theories we studied in class are built on images such as these. Each theory normally identifies a key image for salvation and offers an analysis of the human predicament (guilt, alienation, despair, mortality). My personal rule of thumb is that Christians should have a multifaceted analysis of our condition and be able to use several images for salvation. For example, you found the Greek word *zoe* (life) very interesting. I think Christians need to develop the idea of Jesus as life-giver. Too often the Christian faith is perceived as anti-life, anti-fun, or anti-joy, but Jesus came to offer abundant life, life to its fullest. You might look at 1 Timothy 6:19 for another emphasis on finding true life in Jesus.

If you had to pick your favorite image for Jesus as savior, what would it be? Since Carolyn has an accounting background, she might speak up for the financial imagery (ransom, bought with a price). I'm not sure what a newspaper reporter might like, maybe "good news"?!

From: Chris
To: Dr. Mac
Date: March 23
Subject: Atonement—Reply—Reply

I hope you had a good spring break. You academic types are really lucky. Real working people just get a few weeks of vacation a year! Actually, I'm pretty envious of the academic calendar. I remember how I longed for spring break. Maybe next year Carolyn and I can go as sponsors on our church's ski trip over spring break.

I haven't really decided what is my favorite image for the meaning of the death of Jesus. You're right, the idea of Jesus as life-giver sounds very appealing. I'll keep reading my Bible and look for some of those images you mention so often.

Outside of the Bible, one of my favorite stories with theological themes is C. S. Lewis's *The Lion, the Witch and the Wardrobe.* I reread it recently and was struck by the portrayal of Christ as the lion Aslan. It seems to me that Aslan's death is very close to the New Testament picture of Jesus' death for our sins. Am I on the right track? I'm still not very clear on why Jesus had to die. Couldn't God just forgive our sins?

Oh, by the way, I noticed on our calendar that we are almost to Easter. Maybe this is a good time for me to be thinking about Jesus' death.

From: Dr. Mac
To: Chris
Date: April 6
Subject: Aslan and Atonement

I'm glad you reread Lewis's story about Aslan. I agree that he has given a gripping retelling of the crucifixion. I didn't read Lewis's "children's" stories until I was an adult, and I still enjoy rereading them.

You mentioned some very basic questions in your letter: Why did Jesus have to die? Couldn't God just forgive our sins? Although they are interrelated, let me address them separately. First, some people argue that we don't really know why Jesus had to die. God simply chose that method, and we can't read God's mind. As you might guess, I'm usually pretty nervous about an appeal to mystery. I like paradoxes, but I'm convinced God has given us some clues about the reason(s) for Jesus' death.

Second, be very careful not to isolate Jesus' death from the rest of his life and ministry. One of the traditional ways of developing a comprehensive view of the work of Christ has been to treat the 3 "offices" of Christ: prophet, priest, and king. Most discussions of atonement dwell on his priestly work, since the sacrificial imagery is prominent in the New Testament (Hebrews, especially). Jesus' work as prophet could include his teaching and preaching, and his royal work highlights his announcing of the Kingdom of God. I won't try to map out all of the intricacies of the three offices, but I hope we can put the death of Jesus into a broad context, including all that he came to accomplish through his life, death, and resurrection.

Now, why did Jesus have to die? The simplest biblical answer was in your confession of faith: sin. Your sin. My sin. Yes, religion profs do sin! The Bible often pictures sin as a kind of slavery or bondage. Sin is like an addiction. You may sense something is wrong, but you can't overcome the problem on your own. The Protestant reformers used "total depravity" as the label for this view that we cannot save ourselves. Because Jesus was God's Son, he could do for us what we could not do for ourselves.

Several letters ago I mentioned how much I liked Paul's notion that God was in Christ, reconciling the world. This reminds me that Jesus also died to demonstrate God's love for us. Although I believe in the wrath of God (maybe we ought to look at that sometime), I don't think the Bible portrays God as "mad" at us. God initiates salvation through Jesus. Jesus did not die to appease any angry God who was out to zap us.

Well, I've already started to attempt an answer to your second question. Why didn't God just forgive our sins? I agree that God is a loving, forgiving deity, but love does not equate with an easy-going tolerance. Your experience as a parent might help you here. Although you and Carolyn love your two kids, you have to set some limits in order for them to grow and mature. They can't play in the street! God's love for us is like that. If God simply forgave our sins, it would be easy for us to perceive him as a permissive, grandfatherly kind of God. Please don't let your parents see this *stereotype* of grandparents!

God's forgiveness is costly. To me Jesus' death on the cross is a tremendous demonstration of God's love for us. Jesus' suffering on the cross is a reflection of the pain God feels over our sins. I like the old idea that if you want to know what God looks like, look at Jesus. I stress the continuity between Jesus and God the Father. Without trying to unpack my view of the Trinity, I would emphasize that God "looks like" Jesus. Or, as one preacher put it, Jesus is God's answer to a bad reputation. Jesus' death reminds us that God's love for us is costly.

Maybe one more word picture might help. Some theologians like to use the analogy of a magnifying glass for the relation of God to Jesus. God is present everywhere, but his presence is focused in Jesus. Like a magnifying glass focuses the rays of the sun, so Jesus is the concentration of God's revelation and presence in one human personality. I'm not suggesting that this one image settles all christological and soteriological concerns, but at least it highlights the continuity between Jesus and God the Father. The idea of God being "focused" in Jesus was popularized by J. B. Phillips in his classic, *Your God Is Too Small,* another book you might want to look at.

I hope our correspondence adds to your appreciation of this Easter season. Since I keep referring to the relation of God and Jesus, maybe we need to switch gears to the doctrine of God. The topics of sin and salvation are so intertwined with soteriology, however, you may want to go in that direction. Let me know if you're up to some more correspondence and what topics you want to tackle next.

4

Should We Play God?

From: Chris
To: Dr. Mac
Date: April 16
Subject: In vitro fertilization

I wanted to write to you sooner, but I had postponed doing my income taxes. I thought that legal and financial obligation took precedence over our correspondence! Sorry.

I agree with your comment in your last letter that perhaps we ought to tackle the topics of sin and salvation next since they relate so clearly to my questions about Jesus. But I'd like to change gears for a little while if you don't mind. Last weekend Carolyn and I attended a church "social" (why can't we just call them parties?) and got into a pretty deep discussion with two other couples. Gail and Steve were disturbed at the results from some medical tests they had recently had done. They had been married for seven years and were unsuccessful at having children. The tests revealed a physiological problem, and they now are concerned about how to respond to their infertility.

Well, Gail asked Carolyn and me if we thought it would be all right for them to investigate some options at the infertility clinic at a major research hospital in our town. We hadn't really thought about the issue before, but before we could gather our thoughts another wife, Shelley, said she thought techniques such as in vitro fertilization were wrong for Christians. Couples who tried to conceive that way were playing God, she said. Pretty quickly, several more people got involved in the discussion, and Gail and Steve were really confused by the variety of opinions.

I don't recall the issue of infertility coming up in our theology class. What do you think about methods such as artificial insemination and in vitro fertilization? Are Christians playing God by using technology to try to conceive children?

From: Dr. Mac
To: Chris
Date: April 22
Subject: In vitro fertilization—Reply

I'm glad you got your tax return done on time. My wife usually does our form, and I look it over and sign it. If we think we'll get a refund, she does it early. Otherwise, we get close to the deadline as well.

Your conversation at the church party may become increasingly common. I seem to read a lot about the infertility issue in news magazines. As you might guess, I think the issue is fundamentally a theological one; that is, our view of God affects our decisions about all of life. Let me mention some related issues, and you can follow up.

Some Christians want to start with an examination of biblical texts on conception. Holding to a strong view of the authority of the Bible, they find the passages (and there are quite a few) that mention conception or barrenness. For example, the first conception story in the Bible mentions the role of God; Eve says, "With the help of the Lord I have brought forth a man" (Gen. 4:1 NIV). I often wonder what Adam thought about God getting all of the credit. Other stories, such as Genesis 20:18, mention God causing a woman's infertility.

My concern about interpreting these conception and barrenness stories is that we avoid universalizing or absolutising these stories so much that we say that all conceptions or all infertility is the direct act of God. In other words, I take the infertility issue to be a case study in our understanding of the relation of God to human action. The relationship of divine power and human freedom is what I call an umbrella issue, because it can cover (or be the context) for many specific issues, such as infertility.

Most Christians try to avoid two extremes in this area. One extreme I like to nickname the "Let go, let God" view. Those who absolutise the conception/barrenness stories move in this direction. They stress divine sovereignty or power so much that they would object to technological intervention such as in vitro fertilization. To them, God is the direct cause of fertility or infertility.

The "Let go, let God" view may be true in areas such as salvation (maybe we will get back to that one of these days), but it is really a kind of theological determinism. I know there are several verses that are quoted to support this view, but to me they are taken out of context. A couple of examples. On the surface Exodus 4:11 seems pretty clear: "The Lord said to him, 'Who gave man his mouth? Who makes him deaf or mute? Who gives him sight or makes him blind? Is it not I, the Lord?'" (NIV). The context, however, is God's dialogue with Moses at the burning bush. Moses was reluctant to go back to Egypt to face the Pharaoh, and God was reminding him that He is the ultimate source of power in the universe. In class I sometimes nickname this text the "Helen Keller" passage and ask the students if it really explains her limitations. Of course, a determinist sees no problems with God as the direct cause of blindness, deafness, or infertility. I think God was really trying to get Moses to trust divine resources as he returns to Egypt. Moses wouldn't be on his own.

Another example is Isaiah 45:7. God says, "I form the light and create darkness, I bring prosperity and create disaster;

I, the Lord, do all these things" (NIV). Again, I think the context keeps us from being forced to a determinist reading. Isaiah's concern is to stress the uniqueness of God in a polytheistic environment. God, not the Babylonian or Assyrian gods, is ultimately in control of the world. The "Let go, let God" approach often pushes texts about God's power, omnipotence, toward omnicausality (God directly causes everything).

The other extreme view is what Steve and Gail were concerned about. I think Christians should have a legitimate concern about "playing God." The advent of technology has created a lot of dilemmas for Christians. The more we use technology to solve our problems, the more we face the danger of arrogance. We are increasingly tempted to ignore God and to try to control our lives on our own. The key question is not technological ("*Can* we conceive a child this way?") but theological or ethical ("*Should* we conceive a child this way?").

Well, I realize I've written a pretty long letter. As usual, there are papers to grade. Let me know what you think so far.

From: Chris
To: Dr. Mac
Date: April 28
Subject: In vitro fertilization—Reply—Reply

Your e-mail got my mental wheels turning again. Part of my frustration about questions such as in vitro fertilization is that some of my friends know I was a religion major in college and attended seminary for a while. They think I should have all the answers!

I suppose I assumed that the logical starting point was the specific Bible passages on infertility. I recall you sometimes called that method the "concordance approach" to decision making. You told us to take the Bible seriously but to remember the context for all of those isolated verses.

Carolyn and I must be in the proverbial big, gray middle between the two extremes you mentioned. Our friend Shelley, who objected to using techniques such as in vitro fertilization, must be pretty close to the "Let go, let God" view. She didn't quote any Bible passages, but certainly she thinks God directly controls fertility. "If God wants you to have a baby, you'll have one!" was one of her comments.

Most of our friends at that party had no problems with Christians going to the doctor or dentist when they are sick. Most of us in this middle ground between your two extremes probably use technology to solve some of our problems, yet we still pray for God's help. I suppose we're sort of like the faith-healer in Oklahoma who built the big hospital! Medicine and miracles do not have to be contradictory.

Although I don't recall us discussing infertility in your class, I do remember one example you gave about the use of technology by Christians. You said that class members wearing eyeglasses were making a theological statement! That woke some of us up. Since you wear glasses, you said you were either sinning by opposing God's will for you (poor vision) or exercising his will (using the creativity he gave to humans). I think you said that God's command to Adam and Eve to have dominion over the earth could be used as the basis for the development of technology as well as other forms of human creativity.

Being in the big, gray middle makes me a little nervous. How do Christians decide when the use of technology is appropriate? Incidentally, I noticed you never did really say in your letter whether or not you favor in vitro fertilization.

From: Dr. Mac
To: Chris
Date: May 3
Subject: Bible and Bioethics

I enjoyed your last letter, until the last comment! My students still accuse me of being very slippery about disclosing my personal views. Of course, I tell them that one purpose of my class is to help them think more clearly about the issues, not for me to promote my views. That would be too close to indoctrination in the Big Brother sense. (I presume you're familiar with George Orwell's novel *1984*).

But since you asked.... Let me start with a general answer, and then I'll try to get to a 25-word-or-less answer. Your more basic question was about how Christians decide when the use of technology is appropriate. Your memory is very good about my caution on the "concordance approach" to decision making and my eyeglass example. So many issues in medical ethics, such as in vitro fertilization, are not addressed explicitly in the Bible that many Christians look for general principles.

To help my students in this area, I tried to formulate some biblical principles I thought would help on several of these issues in bioethics. Three of these are:
1. Ultimately, God is the Lord of life.
2. God has given humanity the privilege and responsibility to be wise stewards of life.
3. The current limitations of life will be eliminated eschatologically.

The first two principles were in the background of my earlier letter about the two extreme views ("Let go, let God" and "Playing God"). I believe God is ultimately responsible for the world since he is its creator and sustainer. I do not think he is the direct or immediate cause of everything that happens. To me the key here is the difference between being a "direct" or an "ultimate" cause. The overall teaching of the Bible seems to be that God has left us some elbow-room in the universe. Our task is to be good, wise stewards of the universe, to have dominion over the physical world without dominating or exploiting it.

When a technique such as in vitro fertilization is developed, Christians need to do a very careful theological assessment of it. Some people, like your friend Shelley, are convinced that all conception should occur the "natural" (or perhaps they should say "supernatural") way. Objections to artificial means of birth control follow from this view as well. When I used to teach a Bible study for young married couples, birth control was a common topic. Whether to use artificial means for birth control *or* to use technology to enhance the possibility of conception are two sides of the same theological issue, the proper use of technology by Christians. Since you and Carolyn have two kids, I may be getting into a sensitive area here!

This infertility issue draws together several important theological concerns. I've already mentioned the relevance of your view of God. My second principle mentions our responsibility as humans and hints at the topic of sin (an unwise stewardship of the world). At least two other topics are involved in our discussion. I take infertility to be an example of suffering or theodicy. I know infertile couples suffer a lot of anguish and wonder why they are different. Also, my third principle mentions eschatology, the study of last things (heaven, judgement, return of Christ).

Obviously I can't tackle all of these in a short (?) e-mail, but I did promise you I would give you my answer. I doubt if I can do it in 25 words or less! Overall, I am pretty cautious about new techniques such as in vitro fertilization. Like you, I am in the big, gray middle on questions of medicine and faith. My general principles help me, but they do not dictate a simple answer to a complex issue.

I realize that Gail and Steve will eventually make a "simple" decision, to go to the fertility clinic or not. I would have no objection to a conception occurring "in glass." I would be concerned about how the embryos are used. Are they all implanted in the mother? Are they frozen for later use? Are some destroyed? Frozen embryos or embryos that are destroyed make the procedure much more questionable to me.

Of additional interest to me would be the couple's motive for pursuing in vitro fertilization. Since I don't know your friends, I can't speculate about them. Some people's concern to have "their" child seems self-centered. I wonder how seriously they have considered other options such as adoption. Also, I would be concerned about the expense for such a procedure. Should they use those thousands of dollars for some other purpose?

I suppose my simple answer to the in vitro issue is "maybe." I don't think the biblical/theological principles I mentioned earlier really settle the issue, but they help me lean towards caution. A long time ago I realized that many issues like this one are ambiguous. Indeed, the ability to handle ambiguity is one sign of maturity.

Did you tell your friends that you were consulting an "expert" on this issue? If so, we might look at the issues I skipped over, theodicy and eschatology, before you report back to them. My definite "maybe" is partly based on those issues as well.

From: Chris
To: Dr. Mac
Date: May 10
Subject: Is God just?

Thanks for a long and a "short" answer. Some of us, your students, were curious about your personal opinions. I remember that sometimes you gave them freely, and sometimes you put us off. Perhaps naively we thought all questions had simple answers. Now that I've lived a little longer and experienced a whole lot more I realize how complicated life is. Anyway, I appreciate your "maybe."

I would like to explore with you a little more about the issues of theodicy and eschatology. If I remember right, you told our class that theodicy was the biggest theological issue of all time. That didn't really sink in then. Oh, I learned that "theodicy" is the issue of suffering or evil and that it is based on the Greek words for God and justice. "Is God just?" was your shorthand formula for the issue on tests. Still, my life was pretty calm in those days. My biggest concerns were grades and girls, not necessarily in that order. (I hope Carolyn doesn't read this before I get it sent!) Except for some financial problems, typical of younger couples

I guess, Carolyn and I have faced no major difficulties. Our parents are in good health, our kids are growing like weeds, and we're generally happy with our jobs.

By the way, Carolyn and I have talked to Gail and Steve about their difficulty in having children since that church social, although I haven't told them about my correspondence with you. I'm now beginning to see how disturbed they are by the test results. Also, my work as a newspaper reporter has landed me right in the middle of some of the problems of the "real world." Of course we have stories frequently about tornadoes, disease, divorce, crime, and other kinds of suffering.

Although I can understand the "problem" of suffering better now than in my college days, I'm not sure I have any better answer. What could I tell Gail and Steve about why they are infertile? They're studying some of their options, such as adoption and in vitro fertilization, but they are still struggling with the big "Why?" Why does God let infertility occur?

From: Dr. Mac
To: Chris
Date: May 16
Subject: Is God just?—Reply

I'm glad my attempt at brevity (my "maybe" answer) did not bother you too much. I do believe that brevity is a virtue many church leaders and theologians need to cultivate. Perhaps that's why I ask my theology students to formulate those infamous "25-words-or-less" answers to tough questions.

Your friends are reacting very normally to their infertility. To ask God "Why?" is natural, even for strong Christians. Some of my favorite Bible passages are those dialogues between a human and God. Often those texts are about a perceived injustice in life. If you want some good examples, you might look at Genesis 18 (Abraham and God discussing the destruction of Sodom) or Habakkuk (the prophet and God talk about the invasion of Judah by the Babylonians).

Anyway, I would encourage you to keep on talking to your friends about their concerns. Even though you and Carolyn have children, I don't sense that Gail and Steve feel any resentment or jealousy toward you. But don't feel like you have to have all the "answers" to their questions. Job's "friends" helped him the most when they sat quietly with him. When they began to give their pat, glib answers, they hurt rather than helped. A friend of mine once said the best way to help suffering people is to hush, hug, and hang around. I like that!

One of the most helpful things you might say to Gail and Steve is to remind them that much suffering is not deserved. Most people stress the moral nature of God so much (justice, holiness) that they naturally assume life is supposed to be fair. When an injustice occurs, then we try to find out what we did wrong to deserve this punishment. Let me be clear. I do believe that some suffering is the result of sin. For example, a drunk driver might hurt himself in a car wreck. But he might walk away unscathed while injuring an innocent victim. Gail and Steve may never know why they are infertile (even with extensive medical tests). Ultimately God made a world in which bad things can happen, but assessing blame is often an exercise in futility. You and Carolyn might watch for any signs that Gail and Steve are carrying an unnecessary burden of guilt.

You might also assure them of God's love and concern for them. I know this may seem trite, but in times of suffering we need to go back to the basics. People who suffer often begin to doubt the character of God more than his existence.

Suffering seems to have stages sort of like the stages of grief that psychologists describe. When the suffering is less intense (although I don't believe that "time" heals all wounds), you might be able to discuss the issues with your friends in a more theoretical way. One theologian proposed that there are three stages to suffering. In the first stage the suffering person is often so overwhelmed by the tragedy that she is mute and numb. She may feel powerless and hopeless. In the second stage the suffering person may begin to express concern or even outrage at the evil afflicting them. The biblical psalms includes a lot of laments that reflect this stage of suffering. The third stage involves a more rational, purposive response to the pain. Now the sufferer can begin to accept the problem and begin appropriate problem solving.

Gail and Steve have apparently moved past their initial shock at learning of their infertility. They may still need to ventilate (lament) about their situation at times, but when they make a decision about whether or not to pursue in vitro fertilization they will probably be in the third stage.

One of the difficulties I have teaching on theodicy is that anything I say in a classroom always seems to sound very theoretical. At root, suffering is not an intellectual puzzle. Rather, it is a real life issue, and our response to it needs to be more pastoral than speculative. I'm convinced that a ministry of presence is more important than giving a precise theological answer. A pastor friend of mine once called this ministry "the ministry of showing up." You might be alert to times such as Mother's Day (next week) when Gail and Steve might feel especially down.

Well, I could go on longer on the theodicy issue, but perhaps I've said enough to help a little. If you want to do some reading, C. S. Lewis's *The Problem of Pain* is a classic. Daniel Simundson's *Faith Under Fire* is a helpful survey of the biblical themes.

From: Chris
To: Dr. Mac
Date: May 12
Subject: Is God just?—Reply—Reply

Thanks for your long letter. I especially liked your suggestion about the stages of suffering. Gail and Steve do seem to move back and forth between stages two and three. Sometimes they seem really down, and complain a lot about the unfairness of their situation (stage 2?). At other times, they seem eager to talk about the possibilities of adoption or in vitro fertilization.

I have a copy of Lewis's *The Problem of Pain*, and I'll try to look at it sometime. Recently Carolyn and I checked out the video of "Shadowlands," the Anthony Hopkins-Debra Winger movie about Lewis's marriage. Lewis seemed to be really mad at God after Joy, his wife, died of cancer. Was Lewis experiencing these stages of suffering? Did he have real doubts about God's goodness, or was that theme just a Hollywood spin?

I also wanted to ask you about your third principle on the theodicy issue. How does eschatology relate to suffering?

From: Dr. Mac
To: Chris
Date: May 16
Subject: Shadowlands

I'm glad you looked at "Shadowlands." Although the movie has some factual errors (for example, Joy had two sons from her earlier marriage), I thought the movie accurately depicted some of the theological themes from his experiences with Joy. Lewis did get mad at God when Joy struggled with cancer and died. His book, *A Grief Observed*, is a very candid account of his grief process. I do not think Lewis lost his faith in God, but he certainly struggled with the theodicy issue. The BBC version of "Shadowlands" (with Joss Ackland and Claire Bloom) is better on some of the theology than the Hopkins-Winger version.

The other issue you mentioned, eschatology, is complex, but let me clarify a little what I meant in that general principle: "The current limitations of life will be eliminated eschatologically." The world we live in is not exactly the same world God created. Everything he created was good, but, as some theologians say, we now live in a fallen world. Since God's supreme revelation occurred in Jesus, Christians now live in the tension between the now and the not yet. Salvation is available to us now, but some of the consequences of Jesus' ministry are still to come.

As usual, I see some views to be avoided. On one hand, some Christians believe that *today* we can have most of the blessings promised in the Bible. Some might take this view in a utopian direction, using technology to eliminate evil and suffering. I would argue that we can use technology to solve some of our problems, but the total elimination of suffering in this life is not guaranteed in the Bible. Others might move in a more "spiritual" direction, arguing that the truly pious will prosper. The so-called health and wealth gospel is an example of this approach. Again, this approach is often guilty of proof texting, especially from books such as Proverbs. As a rule of thumb, being pious in the best sense does have positive results (such as a deeper relation with God), but some other passages suggest that being a strong believer might lead to persecution or adversity. I'm thinking of books like 1 Peter or even some of the Beatitudes (Matthew 5:10-12).

On the other hand, some Christians insist that, since suffering is a permanent characteristic of life as we know it now, we should accept our condition as God's will. Such a passive response often leads to a status quo posture that opposes social and technological advances. Since God will remove all suffering at the end of time, any effort to change it now opposes God's will or playing God.

Well, I hope these further musings will help you in your discussions with Gail and Steve. Let me know how their situation develops.

5

What's Wrong With a Mystery?

From: Chris
To: Dr. Mac
Date: May 23
Subject: Summer plans

I talked to Gail and Steve yesterday about some of the ideas in your letters. They were a little surprised that a theology prof was interested in infertility and in vitro fertilization. I assured them that you had always been a little weird! At any rate, they were impressed that academic theology had any relevance to real-life issues. I think they had sort of compartmentalized their life, thinking that their view of God was totally separated from their dilemma about having a child.

Some of your ideas were kind of new to them, so we agreed to talk some more later on. I suggested that they talk to our pastor as well; he seems like a pretty solid guy. He's never mentioned infertility as a sermon illustration, but he might know of others in the church who have wrestled with the issue. It would probably help Gail and Steve to talk to others who have been down this road. I've gradually learned that I need to talk about the big decisions in my life with other Christians. I hope I have the maturity to give Gail and Steve some good advice.

Well, I know the semester is about to end there. What are your plans for the summer? You mentioned that one year you went to England to study. Any trips this summer?

From: Dr. Mac
To: Chris
Date: May 31
Subject: Summer plans—Reply

Good luck with your discussions with Steve and Gail. When I looked back over our recent correspondence, I realized that we had touched on a number of key issues: the nature of God, evil and suffering, eschatology. If you shared very much of our discussion with your friends, they may ask for some course credit!

I wish I had some study trip planned for this summer, but it's my turn to teach summer school. I know people with non-academic jobs always joke about the long vacations we teachers have, but I think I'll stay very busy this summer. Besides summer school, I hope to finish a writing project.

Although I enjoyed dealing with your question about "playing God," I'm afraid I may have left a false impression. I immediately jumped to a pretty abstract discussion of one attribute of God, his power. Of course, itemizing the divine attributes is a traditional way of discussing the nature of God. I felt more comfortable when I suggested that God is like Jesus. I recall you liked my emphasis on "God was in Christ" from Paul. Our discussions of Christology and the doctrine of God need to dovetail somehow so that we remember that we are discussing a distinctively Christian view of God, not some generic god.

When theologians focus on God's attributes, they often talk about two major types. For example, one type includes characteristics such as power, omniscience, omnipresence, eternity, and immutability (unchanging). Contrasted with these so-called "natural" attributes are the "moral" attributes, such as love, mercy, compassion, and patience. Although this classification-of-attributes approach has some real merit, I still have the lingering feeling that the doctrine of God resembles a cook's recipe: a pinch of love, a dash of power, a teaspoon of holiness, and so on. The Bible teaches about all of these attributes, and many more, but it presents God as a living, dynamic reality, not a collage of attributes pasted onto a static background. I like the approach taken by a younger theologian; he organized his discussion under the headings "God is mystery" and "God is love."

Another concern I have with the attributes approach to God is that it often ignores the Trinity. Even though that word does not appear in scripture, I've become convinced that a truly biblical view of God needs to be trinitarian.

So much for the "sermon" or mini-lecture. I hope your summer goes well. Today is my wedding anniversary, and I need to pick up some flowers for Patty. I may not be "Mr. Romance," but I like to do something to commemorate one of the most meaningful events in my life. On our big anniversaries we try to do something special. We took an Alaskan cruise on our 30th anniversary.

Keep in touch, and forgive my professorial compulsion to cram in a few more "points" before the end of the semester.

From: Chris
To: Dr. Mac
Date: June 6
Subject: Trinity

Just a quick note about your last letter. Although I understand your reluctance to dwell on a list of divine attributes, I was a little surprised at your emphasis on the Trinity. As much as you dislike a rationalistic, speculative approach to theology, I didn't expect the stress on the Trinity. Wouldn't it just be easier to think about God as mystery?

From: Dr. Mac
To: Chris
Date: June 13
Subject: Trinity—Reply

I hope your summer is off to a good start. My summer school classes started yesterday. With two classes every morning I'll stay very busy. I enjoy having smaller classes in the summer term, but the pace is very hectic.

Your question (or was it a comment?) about God as mystery deserves a response. I realize I may sound contradictory, but I believe our faith demands that we think of God as a triune being as well as a mystery. I realize that the doctrine of the Trinity, that somehow God is both 3 and 1, sounds like a meaningless intellectual puzzle to most Christians. But the doctrine of the Trinity developed as a legitimate way to point to a distinctively Christian view of God.

Although we hear a lot about how secular people are today, my hunch is that there is still a deep-seated desire for God. A lot of movies, for example, reflect a kind of quest for transcendence, a yearning for a reality beyond the mundane and ordinary. The rash of movies in the last several years about death and afterlife (such as "Ghost," "Always," "Defending Your Life") seem to point to this hunger for the supernatural. The popularity of movies and television shows about angels seems to support that same hunger. "Touched by an Angel" has a very loyal television audience. I really enjoyed the movie "City of Angels" a while back.

Most people believe in God or some kind of supreme being. I suspect that polytheism, not atheism, is the real challenge for Christians today. Many Americans believe in God
(or gods), but their real concern is about God's character.
That's where the Christian view Trinity fits in. To say that
God is Father, Son, and Holy Spirit is another way of saying God is a loving, compassionate reality.

Maybe I'm so emphatic on the Trinity these days because
of a meeting I attended a few years ago. I was invited to be
on a panel to respond to a Muslim speaker. A Roman Catholic, a Methodist, a Jew, and a Baptist (yours truly) were on
the panel. Since I had not studied Islam for awhile, I had to
do some homework! I was reminded that Muslims generally see us as polytheists or tritheists. They believe in one
God, Allah, and argue that Christians believe in three gods.

As it turned out, the Trinity did not become a central focus
of the discussion. Still, I knew the Muslim speaker would
challenge most Christians to be very clear about this 3 in 1
business.

Most Christians seem to solve this dilemma in one of two
ways. First, some are functional unitarians. Excuse the jargon! I mean that they sincerely affirm the official view of
the Trinity, but in ordinary life they tend to focus their attention on either Father, Son, *or* the Holy Spirit. A unitarian of the Father would be like the unitarians of earlier
church history who had rational objections to the Trinity,
sort of like Muslims would. A unitarian of the Son would

be like the Jesus freaks of the early 1970s. They talked so much about Jesus that I sometimes wondered if they believed in or cared about the Father or Holy Spirit. Unitarians of the Holy Spirit would be the "charismatics" who dwell on the power of the Spirit and his gifts. (If you want to see how these three unitarianisms were developed, see an essay by H. Richard Niebuhr that was reprinted in *Theology Today* in July, 1983.)

Second, other Christians see the Trinity like a committee, with God the Father as the chairman. Throughout the centuries he has delegated some duties to the Son and the Holy Spirit, and some he has handled himself. Although some Bible passages seem to support this division of labor, the overall witness of the Bible seems to be that the totality of God is involved in these actions. For example, all three were involved in the creation of the world. Compare Genesis 1 and John 1.

By now you've probably decided that I really am a crusader on this issue! Actually, there are several good ways to describe God without mentioning the Trinity, but I think the notion of Trinity reminds us of important biblical insights into God's nature.

After I send this and have another cup of coffee, I need to get ready for class. Give my best to Carolyn and the kids.

By the way, are you still an avid St. Louis Cardinals fan? I'm not much of a baseball fan, but I check the standings in the newspaper occasionally to see how the Cardinals are doing. I meant to ask you about baseball when the season began, but theology got in the way of sports!

From: Chris
To: Dr. Mac
Date: June 20
Subject: Trinity—Reply—Reply

Yes, I'm still a St. Louis Cardinals fan, although I haven't been able to attend a game in person this season. They're in second place right now, but they're only 3 games out of first.

Now for the serious stuff. I had never really thought of you as a "crusader," although you talked about theology being a passionate discipline. I suppose I find the view of God as mystery appealing because I've never really figured out what the Trinity is all about. The Trinity seems like a concept developed by theologians to confuse lay people! Maybe you've seen the TV commercial where the little boy asks his father where babies come from. The father confuses the boy by using lots of complicated words for sex. I think the father responds, "Under specific ovulatory circumstances a male-female interface may result in an incipient life form that in 9 months. . . ." To me the doctrine of the Trinity, as expressed in the textbooks, sounds a lot like the father's answer!

Your story about the panel discussion with the Muslim speaker helped me understand why you are so strong on this doctrine. I think I saw myself in your unitarianism of the Son category. You remember, I started our correspondence with a question about Jesus. I'll have to work on not ignoring the Father and Holy Spirit.

From: Dr. Mac
To: Chris
Date: June 20
Subject: Mystery

I hope I wasn't so strong on the Trinity that you forgot my emphasis on mystery. I've always loved a good mystery. In fact, my favorite kind of leisure reading is mystery novels. By the way, you might want to look at the Father Brown stories by G. K. Chesterton. Chesterton manages to teach a lot of theology through those tales. I also like Andrew Greeley's novels; they would probably be rated about PG-13, but they also emphasize theological issues well. He's a Roman Catholic priest and sociologist, but I like him mostly for the intriguing stories he tells. If you like historical novels, Ellis Peters's Brother Cadfael stories are great. Cadfael's a medieval monk who solves crimes, and theology sneaks into the plots occasionally.

So, I do like mystery. Sometimes, however, Christians appeal to mystery as an intellectual cop-out. Instead of doing some serious thinking about their faith, they say it's all a mystery.

The word I like even better than mystery is paradox. Several years ago I came across the phrase "logically explorable paradox." Even though I'm not totally sure what that writer intended, the phrase captures what I'm driving at in a lot of my personal theology. God, for example, is ultimately very mysterious, or paradoxical, but he intends for us to use our minds to think about him.

Oh, I have seen that TV commercial about the father explaining babies to his son! I thought it was marvelous. That reminds me that most of my last letter was pretty negative, along the lines of perils to avoid in a discussion of the Trinity. On a more positive note, most Christians have made an honest effort to describe the Trinity through analogies. Some of these comparisons are better than others, but they help keep the Trinity from being an esoteric, abstract concept for us ivory-tower types. Probably the most popular analogy among my last class was the description of one person with three roles: student, daughter, sister. Some students like the water, steam, ice analogy. I still use the children's book *3 in 1* that compares the Trinity to an apple (peel, flesh, core).

Before I forget, one more note about the notion of mystery. Mystery novels always have some clues so that the discerning reader has some chance of figuring out "whodunit." God's revelation of himself in history might be like those clues in the mystery novel. Imagine how frustrating it would be if all of the clues were misleading, and you had no chance at all of solving the mystery. Some interpretations of the Trinity as mystery are like that. In other words, God remains a mystery because God's disclosure of himself as Father, Son, and Holy Spirit is ultimately a series of false, misleading clues. God is not really like Jesus, or Father, or Holy Spirit. Those are merely masks he wore; we can't know the God behind the masks! I fear that such a view takes God to be unknowable or incomprehensible.

To me the thrust of scripture is that the clues, God's revelation in history as Father, Son, and Holy Spirit, are valid pointers to the nature of God. Because he desires a relationship with us, God has revealed himself in a variety of ways. We can't comprehend God completely in this life, but the clues point us to God as he really is. What you see now is what you will see then (more fully and clearly, of course).

Well, enough for now. Soon I will be giving final exams in my summer school classes. If you and Carolyn have a vacation planned this summer and are anywhere near here, come by and see me. If I am not in my office, call me at home. I still live near campus, and we could get together for a visit. E-mail is a wonderful invention, but I still prefer face-to-face conversations.

6

Who Says So?

From: Dr. Mac
To: Chris
Date: July 5
Subject: God told me

Your visit was a very pleasant surprise. I had mentioned our correspondence to Patty, but I had not told her all of the details. Since she has been manager of our campus bookstore for several years, she knows a lot of my students. Sometimes, before they realize who she is, they make some very candid comments about me or my tests! Anyway, she and I were glad you took a break from your trip to see your parents.

Your description of the new pastor in your town was very intriguing. I'm sure interviewing him for your newspaper's Saturday "church page" was quite an experience. The thing you commented on the most was his claim to have visions from God about starting a new church. Although you and I are used to pious people using phrases such as "God told me. . . ," they don't usually claim a direct revelation from God in the sense of an audible voice or vision. After looking awhile I did find that newspaper clipping from a few years ago. Some surveys then said that about a third of Americans testify to "paranormal experiences" such as visions, dreams, or heavenly voices. Maybe the new pastor is not so odd after all.

Although you and I have not had that type of experience, across the centuries some spiritual people, such as mystics, have spoken of such events in their lives. Perhaps what bothers the rest of us is partly the subjective, private nature of those visions. When a famous minister in my state referred to a vision of Jesus, some religious leaders were pretty skeptical.

Traditionally Christians have acknowledged several valid authorities, such as the Bible, experience, church tradition, and reason. Most denominations agree on these authorities, although some debate how they should be ranked in priority. An authority such as a personal experience (visions, for example) is often ranked lower than more "objective" authorities such as scripture or tradition. These authorities are "objective" in the sense that they are outside of us. We might disagree on the interpretation of the Bible, but we acknowledge its authority over our personal opinions.

When a person claims to have talked to God directly, we wonder if he is sane. Older movies such as "Oh, God" and

"Field of Dreams" are based on this predictable reaction to claims of contact with God. Who knows whether someone heard God or his glands? Even Jesus was asked, "By what authority are you doing these things?" (Mark 10:28 NIV).

My hunch is that you reacted so strongly to this new pastor because, like most Christians in our tradition, you place the Bible on the highest level of authority.

Enough follow-up on the shoptalk we did on your visit. Now that summer school is over my schedule will ease up some, but that writing project still beckons me back to my office. I'm glad we got to talk about the Cardinals' season a little while you were here. Hope you got to go to at least one game on your trip.

From: Chris
To: Dr. Mac
Date: July 12
Subject: God told me—Reply

Carolyn and I really enjoyed our brief visit in your home. Our kids are still so young they get restless very quickly. I was glad to see the pictures of your two daughters. I can't believe they're both grown and out of college! Carolyn thought Patty looked a lot younger than you, but I assured her you were in college together and must be about the same age. By the way, we got to see one Cardinals' game, but the second game of the double-header was rained out. I'm not sure the kids would have lasted through two games anyway.

With the busy-ness of our trip, I had not thought too much more about my interview with the new pastor here. He has really made a big splash, and his new church is averaging about 800 in worship.

Although I talked a lot about his "visions," I think my real concern is with his authoritarianism. He was very polite and congenial during the interview, but he seemed very sure that he knew God's will for his church. I remember your wise-crack in class about theocracy. The dictionary definition is the rule of God (or *theos,* if my Greek is not too rusty). If someone proposes a theocracy, you said, then be very sure who "Theo" is. I sense that several religious leaders today are very authoritarian, claiming to be the voice of God. Surprisingly, to me, they are very popular. Some people may be drawn to them because they want a clear, simple (simplistic) answer. Your "definite maybe" about the in vitro fertilization issue would not satisfy them. They want a simple yes or no to all of life's questions.

I remember one class exercise you had us do was rank those authorities (reason, Bible, experience, church, tradition) in order of preference. As you expected, most of the class put the Bible at the top of the list. I guess we are card-carrying Protestants; *sola scriptura* (scripture alone) was one of their themes, wasn't it?

What still mystifies me was that although most of the class put the Bible as the highest authority, we often disagreed on interpretation.

Well, the vacation is over, and I've got to catch up on my work. Thanks again for the hospitality.

From: Dr. Mac
To: Chris
Date: July 20
Subject: Bible

I let Patty see the part of your e-mail reporting Carolyn's assessment of our relative ages! To say she was amused is an understatement.

Let me piggyback on one comment in your letter. You are absolutely right about the disagreement on interpretation of the Bible. One way to try to get a handle on the problem is to realize that we all have acknowledged and unacknowledged authorities. While we all say the Bible is the highest authority for our lives, we are influenced by our age, gender, race, culture, and so on. The fact that I am a middle-aged, middle-class, white, male, Protestant living in the "Bible Belt" affects how I interpret the Bible. In my childhood I learned a song that said, "The B-I-B-L-E, yes, that's the book for me; I stand alone on the word of God, the B-I-B-L-E." As you may recall, I never sang in our class, so maybe I never mentioned that song! Although I still agree that the Bible is the supreme authority, I realize that my interpretation is not totally objective.

By the way, some of the newer trends in theology highlight the influence of race, gender, and culture on our faith. Feminist theologies, black theologies, and a plethora of third world theologies point to the pervasive influence of these factors. In general they insist that much of traditional theology failed to acknowledge these factors and pretended that its interpretation of the Bible was objective.

Some Christians have a hard time sorting out a cluster of issues related to the Bible. Three of the most important are inspiration, interpretation, and inerrancy. Although they are interrelated issues, each deserves careful attention. Inspiration deals with the nature of the Bible and how it came into existence. Interpretation focuses on how we understand that book. Inerrancy highlights the trustworthiness or truthfulness of the Bible.

Well, it sounds like I punched a button and one of my lectures is forthcoming. Forgive me. Even though I'm not in the classroom again until September, it's hard for me to stop being a teacher.

From: Chris
To: Dr. Mac

Date: July 20
Subject: Bible—Reply

Your letter about "inspiration, interpretation, and inerrancy" came soon after our Sunday School class had an animated discussion about the Bible. I don't remember what started it, but the discussion (argument?) was pretty wide-ranging. The class is made up of 7 or 8 young married couples. We're all good friends, but we occasionally have to agree to disagree. I guess we have our own skirmishes in the so-called "battle for the Bible."

Of those three I-words, the one I have the least trouble with is inspiration. You pointed out in class that the Bible does not spell out a specific method of inspiration, but it does affirm the influence of the Holy Spirit on the writers. Exactly how he guided the writers is not clear.

Like a lot of your students, I had grown up hearing the old saying, "The Bible says it. I believe it. That settles it." Still, the issues of interpretation and inerrancy are harder for me to pin down. Any advice?

From: Dr. Mac
To: Chris
Date: August 3
Subject: Interpretation

Your Sunday School class sounds great. At least they seem serious about Bible study, even though there are some disagreements. Some classes spend all of their time discussing sports or television shows and never get around to the Bible.

I think you're on the right track on inspiration. The two most important passages on inspiration are 2 Timothy 3:16-17 and 2 Peter 1:20-21. In 2 Timothy Paul said the Bible was inspired or "God-breathed" without mentioning an exact method. Peter said that the biblical writers were "carried along by the Holy Spirit" (NIV). As you would expect, I like these word pictures, but I don't think they mandate a specific theory of inspiration. Theologians have developed lots of theories about the "how" of inspiration, and some are better than others, but most denominations settle for a simple, basic affirmation of the divine influence on the human writers. The consensus of Christians is that the Bible is a divine-human book, inspired by the Holy Spirit and written by human authors.

To me the other two issues, interpretation and inerrancy, are more complex. Entire books have been written on interpretation. Hermeneutics, or the science of interpretation, can be a very scholarly, sophisticated study. Our Department of Religion recently introduced an entire course on the subject. I usually give a short list of basic guidelines to my freshman classes:

1. Gain a general understanding of the book.
2. Consider the historical background.
3. Use the best text.
4. Use the best translation.

5. Consider the literary form.
6. Follow the guidance of the Holy Spirit.
7. Apply the truth of the text to your life.

Without trying to cram several lectures into a brief letter, I would suggest that many debates about interpretation spring from skipping step one. An old saying claims that you can prove anything from the Bible, but that's true only if you allow proof texting, or taking a verse out of context.

A related concern is what theologians call the "canon within the canon." Because some texts "speak" to us, we assume they are more authoritative and relevant, and we tend to neglect other texts. Gradually we adopt what might be called a "peaks and valleys" approach to the Bible. The peaks are the parts we consider really authoritative (maybe really inspired?). The valleys are the parts of little interest to us. An alternative view is the "flat Bible" view, which insists that all parts of the Bible are equally inspired and equally authoritative.

Across the centuries most Christians land somewhere between these two views. Like the flat Bible view, traditional Christians agree that all scripture is inspired and authoritative. But, like the peaks and valleys view, they also agree that some parts are more relevant today. Following hermeneutical principles such as the ones I listed would help us interpret many passages. Still, I realize that there are no perfect interpreters. Personal and cultural biases affect us all. None of us has the gift of immaculate perception, as I heard it called once!

Let me know if I need to spell out what I mean by hermeneutics a little more. If not, I'll make a stab at the inerrancy issue. A good primer on interpretation is *How to Read the Bible for All It's Worth* by Fee and Stuart. It's one of the textbooks for our new course on "Biblical Hermeneutics."

From: Chris
To: Dr. Mac
Date: August 10
Subject: Interpretation—Reply

Thanks for the list of principles of interpretation. They looked familiar, although I couldn't have reproduced them on a test without some review!

My minor in English had alerted me to some of the difficulties or challenges in trying to understand literature, especially when it's written in another time period and another culture. Without sounding snobbish, I guess I sometimes wondered why other religion majors thought it was so simple to figure out what the Bible said. If Chaucer, Shakespeare, and Milton were hard to read, why should Paul and Isaiah be simple?

Your 5th principle, "Consider the literary form," seems especially crucial for proper interpretation. That the literary form affects the meaning seems obvious, but some people seem to ignore this rule. When Jesus said "I am the gate" or door (John 10:7), he must have been speaking figuratively. One of the running debates in our theology class was about whether the Bible was literally true. That whole debate seemed misplaced to me, since truth can be stated in poetry and parables as well as lab reports about scientific experiments.

I'll try to do some reading on interpretation, perhaps in the Fee and Stuart book, and get back to you when my questions are focused a little more.

I would be interested in your comments on the inerrancy issue. I mentioned to our Sunday School class that I was writing to you. Most of them knew that the original manuscripts of the Bible were lost, so they were curious what inerrancy means for the copies. One member had some "problem passages" as she called them. For example, she mentioned the description of one of the objects in the Temple (1 Kings 7:23). The object was 10 cubits in diameter and 30 cubits in circumference, but pi is not 3.0! She was not denying inerrancy, but she wondered what to do with numbers that contradicted what she learned in high school algebra.

From: Dr. Mac
To: Chris
Date: August 16
Subject: Inerrancy

The inerrancy issue is another proverbial can of worms. Although we don't have the autographs (original manuscripts), most Christians want to affirm the truthfulness of the Bible. Your friend's question about the relationship of the diameter to the circumference is a good starting point. If I were a mathematician, I might be inclined to argue this is an "error" because I would be expecting precise calculations. However, the biblical author is probably using round numbers and did not intend for us to try to construct this object from his approximations. What we count as an error relates very directly to the field of study or application. A draftsman, for example, who is doing blueprints for a construction project needs to be very precise, but an architect might do a rough sketch of what the new house will look like.

A similar example is Deuteronomy 14:12-18, where a bat is classified as a bird! Scientifically a bat is not a bird, but the biblical writer is listing birds that should not be eaten. Apparently his definition of "bird" would be a creature that has wings and flies. Hence, a bat is a bird.

In other places the Bible seems to use observational ("phenomenal" is the technical word) language for scientific topics. The writers describe the world in layman's terms, not with the precision and thoroughness acceptable in your natural science class in college. When, for example, your newspaper reports the times for sunrise and sunset, your readers know that the weather writer is using observational language. Unless some flat earth advocate wants to argue with your paper, the readers accept the theory that the earth is moving around the sun.

Most Christians would agree on the truthfulness of the Bible. Some prefer the word inerrancy; others think the term is unnecessary. Some distinguish types of inerrancy. For example, some say the Bible is totally inerrant or true on all issues (history, science, math, theology, ethics). Others stress limited inerrancy, with the Bible being true on issues of theology and ethics.

Without trying to squeeze too much into a short letter, let me mention two issues related to inerrancy. First, inerrancy is a confusing issue because we aren't always clear on what kind of truth the Bible is presenting. Most books can be classified as either fiction or nonfiction. At least the bestseller lists published in your newspaper follow this division. Where would we classify a parable of Jesus? The genre of parable is probably a form of fiction, yet Christians believe it communicates spiritual truth. Our problem may be that we assume fiction is false and nonfiction is true. Whether or not there "really" was a prodigal son (historical truth), the story is still true (spiritual truth).

Here we see that the inerrancy and interpretation issues are intertwined. Some of my students assume that all inerrantists are also literalists. Although these two views are often held by the same person, they are not the same. An inerrantist might interpret the Bible allegorically or symbolically. Thus, the Bible is completely true, and that truth is communicated symbolically.

Second, we can clarify the truthfulness of the Bible by asking what was the Bible intended to do, or what kind of book is it? My favorite text here is 2 Timothy 3:15-17. Paul said the Bible could "make you wise for salvation" and was "useful for teaching, rebuking, correcting and training in righteousness" (NIV). His primary emphasis is on the theological and moral purpose of the Bible. As one writer put it, the Bible has a "twofold message: (1) how men can be saved, and (2) how saved men are to live." I like that.

I've barely scratched the surface of a tough issue, but maybe you'll be able to make some sense out of these notes. Keep in touch.

From: Chris
To: Dr. Mac
Date: August 22
Subject: Inerrancy—Reply

I shared some of your ideas last Sunday in our Bible study. The regular teacher was on vacation, and she thought the class might be interested in my sharing your views. Most of the class thought your suggestions about round numbers and observational descriptions made sense, but a few thought you had watered down the notion of inerrancy. They wanted to know if these views were fairly standard or if they were your own inventions. I told them that you often told your classes that you had never had an original idea!

Well, I need to do an interview now. I've been waiting two hours to get to meet with the Mayor about her toxic waste program. Thank goodness for laptop computers. I'll send this note soon.

From: Dr. Mac
To: Chris
Date: August 28
Subject: Inerrancy—Reply—Reply

Thanks for letting me know how your class reacted to my comments. You were exactly right: I've never had an original idea, but I do try to borrow from good sources! Do you remember the old saying, "If you borrow from one source, it's plagiarism. If you borrow from several, it's research"?

In just a few days the fall semester will start. I can feel the adrenaline pumping already. Football season can't be far away! Seriously, I really do look forward to the beginning of the school year. As much as I like the extra time for research in the summer months, I enjoy being in the classroom even more.

Let me tie a knot on the end of our discussion of authority. We started with your interview with a pastor who has visions from God. Along the way you mentioned the *sola scriptura* (scripture only) principle of the Protestant Reformation. Although I place the Bible as the highest authority for the Christian life, I like a suggestion by one of my seminary profs. He proposed *scriptura suprema* or the supremacy of scripture as a more accurate depiction of our view. The Bible is our highest authority, but we acknowledge a limited role for other authorities.

Perhaps I need to add one disclaimer here. Ultimately, God is the highest authority for Christians. God has chosen to reveal himself in many ways, and the Bible is the record of that revelation. Therefore, I often call the Bible the highest authority, meaning it is what he has given me to know the most about him.

Perhaps you can work on the notion of a pattern of authority. Beginning with the supremacy of the Bible, what would be the relative authority of sources or influences such as reason, personal experience, church tradition, and the Bible? Some Methodists, for example, refer to the Wesleyan quadrilateral (scripture, tradition, reason, and experience). The pastor you mentioned may talk about the priority of the Bible, but I suspect experiences such as his visions rank very high as well. If his visions ever contradicted a clear scriptural teaching, we could tell where his highest loyalty was.

I hope your newspaper work is going well. Have you had any other interesting assignments lately? Your editor seems to give you a wide range of events and topics to cover.

7

What Is a Human Being?

From: Chris
To: Dr. Mac
Date: September 5
Subject: Ethics committee

Thanks for the new Latin phrase, *scriptura suprema*. I think that does capture the traditional position better than "scripture alone." Even those who insist on the priority of the Bible read it through some filters (race, culture, gender). I haven't totally figured out how the other authorities relate to the Bible (my pattern of authority), so I guess I need to do some more thinking about that.

You asked about my newspaper work. Most of my work is routine: interviews, doing background research, writing articles, and meeting deadlines. But I have had one new development. My editor assigned me the coverage of the hearings of the ethics committee of our state legislature. Although I'll have to commute for awhile, the assignment has been very interesting so far. Most legislative hearings are very boring, but these meetings involve an investigation into improprieties (alleged) in one state senator's office.

I'm not sure if the hearings will lead to a grand jury investigation or not, but so far the evidence seems pretty compelling that the senator did something wrong. Maybe I lean that way because several political figures have been involved in shady deals in recent years. I don't want to sound too cynical, but the lack of integrity in public life seems to have reached epidemic proportions lately. I think the general public has almost come to expect these leaders to play dirty. Of course, a few years ago revelations about indiscretions by religious leaders made the front pages of most newspapers as well. Sometimes I wonder how people mess up so royally.

I trust your semester has started off well. At times I wish I were back in school. Most students in my generation didn't seem to realize how good they had it!

From: Dr. Mac
To: Chris
Date: September 13
Subject: Ethics committee—Reply

Your new assignment does sound interesting. Like you, I've noticed an unusual number of instances of what someone called "the integrity crisis" recently. Political and religious leaders are not the only ones who mess up (royally?), but their visibility as public figures makes them more vulnerable to scrutiny by the media. Don't take that last comment personally. I guess bad news such as crime, corruption, or scandal is still more newsworthy than so-called good news. Who would be interested in headlines such as "Pastor Jones Remains Faithful to Wife" or "Governor Lopez Is Honest Again"? When a leader stumbles, that's news.

I didn't think you sounded particularly cynical about human nature in your last letter. Christians are often accused by outsiders of being pessimistic about human nature. Our notions of original sin, total depravity, and so on seem overly negative to some. I suspect that one reason humanism has been attractive to many is that it acknowledges the accomplishments of humanity.

As a theologian I think "sin" is a meaningful term for one aspect of the human condition. When my colleagues from other disciplines discuss the causes of problems like world hunger, war, or poverty, I always mention sin as a factor. I think the social sciences, for example, are very helpful in understanding what makes us tick, but the theological dimension needs to be included in the discussions. I was a psychology major in college, but I fear a reductionistic approach to human questions and answers. Reductionism might be nicknamed "nothing-but-ism," since it says humans are nothing but genetic codes (or environmental influences). I have been interested that some social scientists have recently taken the traditional seven deadly sins as a focus for discussion.

Good luck on your reporting on the ethics committee. Maybe some of your reports will be picked up by the wire service and make their way into our paper.

From: Chris
To: Dr. Mac
Date: September 19
Subject: Sin

My coverage of the ethics committee investigations is still keeping me busy, but I wanted to drop you a short note while the committee has recessed for lunch. My assignments in the last few months have tended to be on crime or other types of bad news, and I have let myself dwell on the dark side of human behavior. My newspaper, like most, sees some events (usually bad) as more newsworthy, but we do run the occasional human interest story to try to give some "good news."

Let me mention one question that you might want to follow up on. If, as you said, "sin" is a useful way of analyzing human behavior, why do we sin? Our educational system seems to be based on the premise that when we know the right thing to do, we will do it. Indeed, what bothered a lot of the public about some of the recent scandals was that the criminals/sinners were lawyers, doctors, ministers, and other highly educated professionals. Although some of these educational institutions have added courses on ethics, I wonder if that will prevent the corruption from occurring again. The Nike ads on TV tell us "Just do it!"

The committee is ready to begin for the afternoon session. At least with my laptop computer I can check e-mail and work while I'm on the move.

From: Dr. Mac
To: Chris
Date: September 28
Subject: Sin—Reply

I saw a brief report on the TV news about the ethics committee hearings and thought I saw you in the press section. It sounded like the committee will issue its report by next week.

Your question about why people sin has a simple (or simplistic?) answer, temptation. Of course, it's not automatic that the tempted person will sin, so the issue is really more complex. Christians insist that Jesus was tempted, but he did not sin.

A related question that perplexes some people is the source of temptation. A few suggest that God is the source of temptation since he is the sovereign of the universe. Most Christians, however, use James 1:13 as a refutation of this notion: "For God cannot be tempted by evil, nor does he tempt anyone" (NIV). Certainly God created a world in which we face choices about good and evil, but he does not directly tempt us.

More often Christians talk about Satan or the Devil as the source of temptation. One of my favorite C. S. Lewis books, *The Screwtape Letters,* is a fictional correspondence between a senior devil and a junior devil about the art of temptation. Although Satan is not mentioned much in the Old Testament, he is discussed frequently in the New Testament. Paul at times describes the Christian life as a spiritual war. Ephesians 6:10-20 describes this warfare and our spiritual armor. When we sin, one excuse we often make is "The Devil made me do it."

I've noticed that several church leaders talk a lot about the spiritual warfare image. Some recent "horror" or suspense movies have dealt with demons, demon possession, exorcisms, and related topics. I fear we may be giving the Devil too much attention or credit. The Bible is very clear that Satan is a created being and is not equal to God. To stress Satan's power, for example, borders on the dualism of some ancient religions. The New Testament stresses that God has defeated Satan, not that they are mirror images engaged in an eternal conflict.

When I face temptation, two other influences are more obvious to me. First, some of my desires get me into trouble. I want to be careful here. I don't mean that desires in and of themselves are bad. I like the old definition of sin as the illegitimate expression of a legitimate desire. James 1:14-15 highlights this scenario: desire—> sin —> death. Every time I work at my computer keyboard I have to resist a desire to visit the ice cream store I can see from my office window! Hunger is a good desire, but gluttony is a sin! Yes, I still have frequent cravings for a banana split at that ice cream store.

Second, some temptations come from other people. Paul mentioned this source in 1 Corinthians 15:33. "Bad company corrupts good character" (NIV). Of course, the wisdom literature of the Old Testament, especially Proverbs, stresses associating with the right kind of people. I am not often tempted to commit a "big" sin because of peer pressure; after all, I work in the Department of Religion! Still, it's easy for me to join in too many coffee breaks or fritter away my time on inconsequential activities. My sins, whatever the source, are often sins of omission rather than sins of commission (doing a bad deed). James 4:17 is the classic description of a sin of omission, knowing the right thing to do and not doing it. Incidentally, there is a good book on this topic, *Sins of Omission: A Primer on Moral Indifference* by S. Dennis Ford.

Before I confess any actual sins, I'd better pack my briefcase and take some papers home for late night grading.

From: Chris
To: Dr. Mac
Date: October 3
Subject: Sin—Reply—Reply

Your e-mail about temptation came just as I finished my reporting on the ethics committee hearings. You probably read that the ethics committee found evidence of real problems in the senator's office and have recommended a grand jury study. If I were a betting person, I'd bet there is an indictment by Thanksgiving.

Thanks for the brief discussion of the source of temptation. For a while I thought you might actually confess some sin! Seriously, I wondered why you didn't mention Adam and Eve in your comments. Maybe they would fall under the heading of "other people" as the source of temptation, but your example there was peer pressure. Don't most denominations link our sins to the sin ("the Fall") of Adam and Eve in some way?

I guess I thought of Adam and Eve partly because of our pastor's children's sermon last Sunday. Kevin, our oldest, is big enough now to join the other kids for this "sermon." Of course, the adults listen carefully as well. At any rate, our pastor told the story of Humpty Dumpty and compared it to the sin of Adam and Eve. He didn't use the jargon of original sin and total depravity, but he was teaching those concepts. I vaguely remember that you used to do children's sermon's.

By the way, I learned recently that I will be assigned to report on our denomination's state convention in November. I attended one session when I was in college, but basically it will be a new experience for me.

From: Dr. Mac
To: Chris
Date: October 10
Subject: Original sin

If I read your e-mail correctly, you asked two questions, one easy and one hard. The easy one was about my having done children's sermons. Yes, while I was in graduate school I led children's worship services as part of my duties on a church staff. Later on, I occasionally did some children's sermons in the church I attend here. You may have noticed the picture of Dr. Seuss on my office wall! In these "sermons," I usually tried to correlate a Dr. Seuss story with a spiritual truth. Sometimes that was a real stretch! I also have a poster for Seuss's *The Butter Battle Book* in my office. Some of the Seuss stories are just "fun," but many have a clear moral message. I especially like the ones that are open-ended, such as *The Lorax* (about ecology), or have a strong ethical slant, such as *The Sneetches* (about discrimination).

Your hard question was about the relationship of the Fall of Adam and Eve to our sins. You're right that most Christian groups have seen some connection there. The old Puritan saying "In Adam's fall we sinned all" might be interpreted in several ways, and denominations have disagreed on the exact nature of the link.

"Original sin" is the traditional nickname for this topic. Most people in our tradition would stress a strong connection between the first sin and our sin. Some would argue that the biological link is essential. Because we are the descendants of Adam and Eve, we share in their sin and guilt. Sin is transmitted biologically throughout the human family tree, and we are all born sinners. The most famous passage used to support this view is probably Romans 5. Paul compares the impact of Adam and Christ on human history. Sin entered human history through one man, Adam (v.12). Christ made salvation available (v. 18).

This traditional view has been criticized by many theologians and denominations for its emphasis on biological inheritance. Instead of this "natural headship" view, which stresses the biological link between us and the first couple, some prefer a "federal headship" view in which Adam is our representative. Just as the Governor or the President acts as my representative, even if I did not vote for her, her actions impact me. Some argue that this view would allow for a symbolic reading of Genesis 3. Adam would be Mr. Everyman, representing or symbolizing the spiritual truth that we all "fall."

One reason I did not mention Adam and Eve in my earlier letter is that this discussion can get very speculative. At root it is a hermeneutical or interpretation issue. Most Christians are more concerned about how to handle the temptations they face daily than about where sin came from originally.

Another concern for me is that some of these older discussions bog down in debates about the inheritance of the soul and/or body from Adam and Eve. One view, known as traducianism, says that we inherit our soul and body from the original pair. Another view, creationism, says we get our body from that pair but that God creates a new soul for each of us and implants it in the womb as we develop. My concern is that this soul/body discussion borders on a dualistic separation of human nature into two distinct parts. Although scholars debate the issue, many insist that the Bible has a unitary or holistic view of human nature. Even when terms such as soul, body, and spirit are used, they refer to dimensions or aspects of human nature, not totally separate parts. A very interesting book is *Body, Soul, and Life Everlasting: Biblical Anthropology and the Monism-Dualism Debate* by John W. Cooper.

Well, I've dropped a lot of jargon again. Most of it you heard in our theology class, but it's not common parlance for most people.

I was glad to hear you will cover the state convention. Sometimes it's pretty routine, with many reports and sermons. Every now and then something controversial happens. A little controversy would probably be more newsworthy for you, but I usually like the quiet ones. I don't know if I will be there or not. I usually try to make at least one session and attend the reception for our alums.

From: Chris
To: Dr. Mac
Date: October 18
Subject: Original sin—Reply

Your last letter made me feel like I was back in one of your theology classes! I recall that some days you almost overwhelmed us with new concepts or at least new terms for familiar ideas. Typically one of us would ask, "Will that be on the test?" You always said, "Maybe." If you had said, "No," then we probably wouldn't have studied it.

Another common reaction to the complexities of theology was "So what?" Sometimes it was hard for us to see the practical relevance of these theological debates to our everyday lives or our ministries. Your response on the soul/body issue was pretty good. I found a simple chart in the margin of my textbook for that course.

HOT GOSPEL:
individuals   spiritual needs (soul)   evangelism

SOCIAL GOSPEL:
groups   physical needs (body)   social ministry

You said that some Christians stress the spiritual needs of individuals and others stress social problems. Most of the class thought evangelism was the central task of the church and individual Christians, but a few thought we ought to spend more time addressing issues such as poverty and racial discrimination. Pretty quickly we saw the practical relevance of these issues.

I do hope to see you at the state convention. If the alumni reception doesn't conflict with a deadline, I'll try to be there.

From: Dr. Mac
To: Chris
Date: October 27
Subject: Hot gospel

I didn't know exactly how the discussion on hot gospel/social gospel went in your class, but I've used that little diagram for several years. I usually conclude by saying that a balanced view of human nature and our ministry needs to include both aspects, what has been nicknamed the "whole gospel." Our denomination has usually been stronger on the hot gospel, but several of our agencies strive to deal with social needs as well.

When I teach that theology course each year, I can usually predict what issues will interest the students the most.

Natural headship and federal headship have not been real
attention grabbers lately!

The topic of the creation is a perennial winner. Usually I
just present the basic issues and then referee the discussion. Although all of my students believe that God created
the world, they disagree on some of the details. A few still
think the issue is creation vs. evolution, but they soon realize how complex it really is.

The Bible is clearer on the "who" and the "why" of creation than on the "how" and the "when." As the old creed
says, God is the maker of heaven and earth. Although the
Bible does not give an explicit reason why he created the
world, many theologians argue he created the world and
us for fellowship with him.

The "when" question seems to be answered in Genesis 1
with the frequent references to "day." Whether God created the world in six days of 24 hours or over a long period
of time is one of those classic interpretive debates. The
young earth advocates insist the world is only a few thou-
sand years old. The old earth advocates suggest that the
universe could be billions of year old.

The "how" question is also a hot topic in my classes. Genesis 1 pictures God speaking the world into existence, sort
of like a military leader barking out orders. Genesis 2 portrays God more like a potter or sculptor as he creates man
from the dust. Whether these images are literal or figura-

tive is crucial to the discussion.

Sometimes my students get so wrapped up in the debates about creation that they overlook the stress on the dignity of humanity in Genesis 1 and 2. I really like the emphasis on our being created in the image of God. I'll sound like a broken record, but there has been a lot of debate about what that is exactly. I'm not sure whether it's reason, the soul, our dominion over the world, or our capacity to relate to God, but it sets us apart from the rest of creation.

Since Christians affirm the universality of sin and our need for salvation, we sometimes forget this positive side to the biblical portrait of humanity. As sinners, we might resonate with the psalmist's "But I am a worm and not a man" (Ps. 22:6 NIV). Another psalm highlights God's concern for us:

"[W]hat is man that you are mindful of him,
the son of man that you care for him?
You made him a little lower than the heavenly beings
and crowned him with glory and honor." (Ps. 8:4-5 NIV)

We Christians often discuss sin so much that we let others, such as the humanists, get a corner on the positive side of human nature.

Since you graduated, I've started using an outline I call the "stages of humanity" to illustrate the overall biblical witness on human nature. Of course, I use the term "man" in a generic sense!

ESSENTIAL MAN: image of God
EMPIRICAL MAN: sinful man
ESCHATOLOGICAL MAN: redeemed man

Christian humanists would stress the first stage, while ministers and theologians often highlight our fallen state. Our hope as Christians is that we can be reconciled with God through Jesus.

Well, I need to look through some commentaries. I'm trying to write a new sermon outline for Sunday. I could pull an old outline out of the file, but I do occasionally write new ones.

Sorry I kind of rambled in this letter. So many of these issues are interrelated that I have a hard time separating them.

8

Are You in Step With the Spirit?

From: Chris
To: Dr. Mac
Date: November 2
Subject: Charismatic

I was a little surprised that you could predict what topics would be most interesting to your students; I didn't realize that college students were so predictable! I know that some topics in theology were more interesting to me and most of the class than other issues. Like most students, though, I remember some of your stories better than the regular lectures. You usually said those stories were "meaningful digressions," not rabbit chasing!

Your comment about not letting the humanists corner the market on the positive side of human nature hit home with me. Some Christians (like me?) emphasize negative human behavior so much that we give a one-dimensional view of human nature. A Christian perspective is actually very realistic about human nature. We are created by God, in his image, yet we became sinners. I'm glad you mentioned the 3 "stages" of humanity outline. In my Shakespeare class in college we read about the 7 "ages" of man in "As You Like It." In my psychology classes we learned about the typical developmental stages of humans. So, I was interested that some theologians have a chronological scheme as well.

A quick story before I head to my next assignment. Last weekend Carolyn, the kids, and I visited Carolyn's parents to celebrate Angela's second birthday. While all the cousins played, I broke one of my cardinal family rules: Don't discuss politics or religion at a family get-together. Carolyn's Aunt Eileen seemed pleased that Carolyn and I had become active in our church again. She seemed very curious about what kind of church it was and asked lots of questions about our programs. To make a long story short, she eventually asked about our church's views on the Holy Spirit. I couldn't recall any sermons or Sunday School lessons recently on the Holy Spirit, so I gave a few general comments about the Holy Spirit inspiring the Bible and helping us be better Christians.

Aunt Eileen got pretty frustrated at my answer. "Don't you all believe in the spiritual gifts?" she asked. I tried to assure her that we did believe in the power of the Holy Spirit, but she thought I was being evasive. Well, somehow I excused myself, probably to go "check on the kids." On the drive home, I asked Carolyn about her aunt. Carolyn said that Aunt Eileen had attended a Methodist church most of her life (she's about 55 years old), but about 3 years ago she had joined a "charismatic" church. (I had to use the quotation marks because I know you insist that all Christians are charismatic in the biblical sense.) I don't think I burned any bridges with Aunt Eileen, yet I felt really awkward trying to discuss the Holy Spirit. Like I said in an earlier letter, perhaps I've been guilty of a unitarianism of the Son. I've neglected thinking much about the Holy Spirit.

Well, I must get to that assignment. Do you know yet if you'll be at the state convention in a couple of weeks?

From: Dr. Mac
To: Chris
Date: November 8
Subject: Charismatic—Reply

Yes, I think I'll be able to attend part of the state convention next week. I skipped a professional meeting earlier this fall, so I can afford to call off classes one day. My students deserve a break occasionally, or so they tell me. I hope we can get together at the alumni reception on Tuesday night.

I'm not surprised at Aunt Eileen's reaction. The "charismatic" movement has been very strong in recent years. I'm afraid most of our churches try to avoid too much discussion of the Holy Spirit, lest we look "charismatic." I do still insist that all Christians are charismatic in the biblical sense of being gifted by the Holy Spirit. Unfortunately, if I said I were charismatic in some of our churches, they would assume I spoke in tongues, practiced faith healing, or handled snakes.

I recently started using a little diagram I based on a reference book article to illustrate the variety of positions held by Christians on the spiritual gifts, especially speaking in tongues. First the chart, then a little explanation.

Are tongues available now? Are tongues the ideal today?

Positive	Yes	Yes
Negative	No	No
Mediating	Yes	No

I kid my students that I got a Ph.D. to think up outlines like that! The positive school would be the "charismatic" perspective. They insist that all of the spiritual gifts (*charismata*) listed in texts such as 1 Corinthians 12-14 and Romans 12 are available today. Gifts such as speaking in tongues are to be sought or cultivated for a fully spirit-filled Christian life.

The negative school generally holds that tongues ceased in the first century. They use 1 Corinthians 13:8 to prove that tongues were temporary. In the first century tongues helped authenticate the early Christian movement, but now that we have the canon of scripture, they argue, we don't need tongues.

The mediating school agrees that all of the spiritual gifts are available to us today. They do not elevate gifts such as tongues to a higher rank. Indeed, one slogan they use is "Seek not, forbid not."

My hunch is that many churches in our denomination are in the negative camp, but some are open to the mediating view. Occasionally I read in our denominational newspaper that a church has been criticized or even excluded from membership over this issue. Our official confession of faith does not address the tongues issue explicitly, although it does mention the spiritual gifts briefly. I think the authors of that document may have included some planned ambiguity in order to allow for some diversity. Still, a lot of our churches are suspicious of the charismatic movement.

Over the last few years, however, I have been taking an opinion poll in my theology classes. I ask, "Which of these 3 views does our denomination hold?" At first, most of my Baptist students placed us in the negative camp. Now a lot of my Baptist students think we are "mediating." Our denomination may be moving on this topic!

I look forward to seeing you at the convention, if your deadlines allow.

From: Chris
To: Dr. Mac
Date: November 15
Subject: Convention debate

Just a short note. I just got some particulars on what my editor wants me to do at the state convention. Barring an emergency, I'll be at the alumni reception.

I've called some of the convention leadership to set up interviews between the sessions, and I thought you might be interested in one lead I got. Dr. Smathers indicated that they anticipated that a leading pastor in our state would propose a resolution criticizing the "charismatic" movement. Apparently he believes some of our churches are too "soft" on the issue of tongues. Dr. Smathers is hoping that a controversy will not develop. Apparently another pastor will propose that a task force be appointed to study the issue thoroughly and report back at next year's convention.

As a newspaper reporter I have mixed feelings. A heated discussion on the floor of the convention would make for bigger headlines. As a member of this denomination, however, I hate to see any issue become divisive. We've seen a lot of controversy already!

I suppose many of our churches, or their pastors, would be in the negative school you mentioned in your letter. I really don't know where my church would be. The issue hasn't turned up in our Sunday School class lately.

Oh, if the task force is appointed to study the tongues issue, is there any chance you would be on it? Anyway, see you at the reception.

From: Dr. Mac
To: Chris
Date: November 22
Subject: Convention debate—Reply

I really enjoyed visiting with you at the convention. I get to see some former students who serve on church staffs in our state. Some of them can't come to Homecoming and the state convention. Occasionally, they even ask me to come speak in their churches.

I'm glad the convention decided to appoint the study group on tongues rather than trying to thrash out a complex issue as a committee of the whole (1500+ in this case). Of course, when the task force reports back next year, we may have that kind of debate anyway.

I think the membership of the task force is good, even though I wasn't named to it. Our denomination rarely asks "professional" theologians to be on groups that deal with theological issues. I used to be sensitive about that, but I really do believe that all of us are theologians. I usually start my theology classes by insisting that my students were theologians before they ever enrolled in my class. Of course, Karl Barth reminded us that we are all "little theologians." Since I get paid to teach theology, I'm a professional. All Christians have an obligation to think carefully about their faith, so we're all theologians.

Ideally, this task force will put the tongues issue in the larger context of the doctrine of the Holy Spirit. Although the New

Testament deals several times with tongues, most prominently in 1 Corinthians 14 and Acts 2, the work of the Holy Spirit is varied. Besides inspiring the biblical authors and guiding us as we try to interpret it (usually called illumination), he is involved in activities such as the creation of the world and strengthening us in our Christian pilgrimage.

When I start the unit on the Holy Spirit in class, I usually ask the students to think of the most "spiritual" person they know personally. I don't want them to give personal names, lest they embarrass someone! Frequently the answers point to people who have had unusual, even ecstatic experiences. Spiritual gifts such as tongues or healing are sometimes mentioned, but more often I hear about vivid, "mountain-top experiences."

Since I also teach an ethics course, I try to balance the discussion by introducing a saying I heard years ago, source unknown: "The real evidence of the Spirit is not how high you jump but how straight you walk when you land." I don't mean to set up a false dichotomy between emotion and ethics, but I want my students to notice the biblical emphasis on the moral behavior of people who are "in the Spirit."

One of my favorite passages on the Holy Spirit is Galatians 5:16-26, where Paul contrasts life in the flesh and life in the Spirit. Rather than seeing flesh and spirit as two parts of human nature, I think Paul intended two value systems or belief systems. A Christian is to act and think differently.

Commentators usually classify the works of the flesh (vv. 19-21) as a vice list and the fruit of the Spirit (vv.22-23) as a virtue list.

Although the tongues issue is a serious one, I hope the task force provides a large context in its report and helps educate our people on the overall work of the Holy Spirit. Many of our churches simply neglect the topic. Such a vacuum in preaching and teaching makes it easy for misunderstandings to develop. The doctrine of the Holy Spirit, like all of the major doctrines, should be a regular topic in proclamation and education programs.

I'm grateful next week is a short class week. I know my students are ready for Thanksgiving, even though a few will need to work on their research papers. Those papers are supposed to be "term" papers, meaning they work on them all term long. Realistically, however, I realize that some of my students will crank out weekend wonders for me.

From: Chris
To: Dr. Mac
Date: November 30
Subject: In step with the Spirit

I got your e-mail just in time! Carolyn and I had decided to go visit my parents for Thanksgiving. My hometown pastor invited me to speak to the college Sunday School department on the Sunday after Thanksgiving. He really hopes that some day I'll return to seminary and get back into the ministry! Since we had been discussing the Holy Spirit, I thought I might talk about that topic. Our correspondence about the tongues issue and the state convention were fresh on my mind, but I didn't want to tackle the tongues issue yet. I had not come up with a good text, but I decided ("felt led") to use that Galatians passage.

The part I really emphasized was in verse 25: "Since we live by the Spirit, let us keep in step with the Spirit" (NIV). I used a marching band analogy to introduce the importance of keeping in step. By the way, I remember when you and some other teachers had the "Fighting Faculty Marching Band" during the halftime of the Homecoming basketball game several years. Most of you played kazoos, but you played (?) the cymbals. The students really enjoyed the effort, even though the musical quality was not very high. Anyway, several of the college students had been in band and liked the illustration. If I had any military experience, I could have used learning to march in boot camp as an example of marching.

I don't have a manuscript of what I said, but I did have three "points." First, being in step with the Spirit might mean being out of step with your culture. I used the famous quotation from Henry David Thoreau: "If a man does not keep pace with his companions, perhaps it is because he hears a different drummer." My main illustration was the movie "Witness." Carolyn and I had seen the video recently.

Harrison Ford played a big-city cop who lives with some Amish while he investigates a crime. The movie really highlights the clash of the different value systems. Ford's character was used to using violence to solve problems, and the Amish were pacifists. Talk about a culture clash!

Second, being in step with the Spirit means all of your life is guided by the Spirit. I liked your idea that there is no radical separation of the physical and the spiritual. We are to honor God with our total beings.

Third, being in step with the Spirit does not mean Christians are exactly alike. The danger of my marching band introduction was that it left the impression we all wear the same uniforms and march lockstep. I like the saying, "We can be brothers without being twins." If I had had more time I could have developed this point with Paul's teaching on the diversity of the spiritual gifts in 1 Corinthians 12.

I got a pretty good response to my three points. Who knows, if I ever get asked to preach again I could turn that outline into a regular sermon.

Life will be hectic for the next several weeks. Sunday was the first Sunday in Advent. Carolyn and I have decided to use an Advent wreath to help Angela and Kevin learn more about the real meaning of Christmas. We're still discussing where to spend Christmas. We usually spend the big holidays with either her parents or mine. Since we spent Thanksgiving with my folks, I guess we'll go to her folks.

The thought of staying here and not traveling anywhere is attractive. What do you and Patty do about traveling on holidays? I presume you've worked out a satisfactory solution.

9

What Must I Do to Be Saved?

From: Dr. Mac
To: Chris
Date: December 6
Subject: In the Spirit

I really enjoyed reading the summary of your devotional on keeping in step with the Spirit. If I ever "borrow" it I'll give you credit! One reason I like to read new Bible translations is that I notice insights that I often overlook in more familiar versions. The marching band image fits in very well with the NIV's keeping in step translation.

Without trying to improve or change your outline, a 4th idea occurred to me. A Christian could be "in the Spirit" without being in step with the Spirit. At least Paul often encourages his readers to be active in expressing their faith in concrete ways. Scholars sometimes note Paul's use of the indicative and the imperative. In effect Paul says to be what you are: "You are a Christian (indicative), so act like it (imperative)." Some more evangelistic denominations have emphasized the instantaneous nature of salvation (conversion, born again), but in recent years some of these groups have increasingly stressed the need for growing and maturing as a Christian.

I suppose I was reminded of all of this by two recent events. One was my preparation to teach an ethics course in our January term. The course is one of my favorites, but some students aren't so sure Christians need to study ethics. They seem to think, "When we're saved, our nature is changed. Why do we need to study ethics?" One way I respond to that concern is by using some of the ideas from the recent rediscovery of character and virtue by scholars. Character and virtue haven't been "lost," but some scholars have a new emphasis on these topics! Our character and positive habits (virtues) need cultivation over time. Conversion does change us, but for most of us there is a lot of growing to do. We're baby Christians before we are mature Christians. The writer of Hebrews stressed the need for practice or training in moral discernment (5:13-14).

The other event was a business meeting at my church last month. Our Evangelism Committee recommended a time and speaker for our annual revival next fall. Although that kind of motion usually passes without any discussion, this time a few people asked if a revival was a good idea. After about 20 minutes of discussion, we decided to try a "discipleship" conference instead of the revival as our special event for the fall. One member noted that he wasn't against evangelism, but he thought a discipleship conference would benefit us more.

These two events reminded me that Christians need some help and encouragement in maturing or growing up in Christ. A Christian is a "new creation" (2 Cor. 5:17 NIV), but we are often babes in Christ (1 Cor. 3:1). Ethical instruction in a college classroom and a discipleship conference at a church are good ways to encourage growing up as Christians.

Oh, you asked about how Patty and I decided where to spend holidays like Christmas. Early in our marriage we decided to stay at home for Christmas. We wanted our kids to develop their own Christmas traditions. We've used the advent wreath with some success. Our girls really liked their advent calendars as well.

I hope you have a very happy holiday season. Oh, do you still follow college basketball? Our men's team is struggling a little, but the women's team is still undefeated. Of course, the season is young, but I think that both teams have a chance at getting to the national tournament again.

From: Chris
To: Dr. Mac
Date: December 13
Subject: Salvation

Thanks for letting me know what your family does about travel for the Christmas season. Carolyn and I haven't totally decided what to do yet. As long as I am the new kid on the block, my work schedule may settle the issue for us!

I'm glad the basketball teams are winning. I attended most of the home games when I was a student. I remember seeing your family and some other profs in the reserved section. You were usually more animated during the games than in the classroom!

Your church's discussion about whether or not to have a revival reminded me of some of the dorm bull sessions I used to be in. One time the guys in the dorm went round and round about the value of the evangelistic services at our summer camp. Some of the ministerial students defended them because so many teenagers made decisions for Christ. A few argued that many of these decisions were emotional responses and not true life-changing commitments. We could all remember how tough it was to return to our home towns and leave the emotional (spiritual?) high we had felt at camp.

Although the term "discipleship" was used some when I was at college, I heard even more in that one year I went to seminary. I know "disciple" means something like learner or follower, but I wasn't really sure what all it implied. Although I never took your ethics course, I guess I must have had a little of the negative attitude you mentioned. If Christ has saved us, why don't we just act right? I've heard some testimonies of people who experienced dramatic changes, such as an alcoholic losing the desire for alcohol immediately.

Maybe I'm a little confused on the issue of salvation in general. Can you give me one of those 25-words-or-less definitions you used to ask us to write?

Have a good Christmas season.

From: Dr. Mac
To: Chris
Date: December 19
Subject: Salvation—Reply

I don't know if I can do justice to any theological topic in 25 words or less! I hope that's not a cop-out. One problem is that, since our decision not to have a revival next fall, my pastor asked me to teach a Sunday night series on the doctrine of salvation. He wasn't particularly bothered about the discussion at the business meeting, but he felt this might be a "teachable moment" for a fuller discussion of how evangelism, conversion, revivals, and discipleship all fit together. All that is to say I've been trying to pull together some notes and outlines for that series, as well as get ready for Christmas and my January term class.

For me the easiest way to summarize an evangelical view of salvation is to refer to 2 sides to salvation and 3 stages of salvation. The 2 sides are grace (the divine initiative) and faith (the human response). One of the best passages to illustrate this is Ephesians 2:8-9.

"For it is by grace you have been saved, through faith—
and this not from yourselves, it is the gift of God—
not by works, so that no one can boast." (NIV)

Both of those key terms deserve careful study, but let me
try for brevity.

Grace is a gift from God. The first definition I ever learned
for "grace" was "God's unmerited favor." I also like Paul
Tillich's emphasis on "you are accepted." A lot of people
feel unacceptable—either to themselves or others. God's
grace is his forgiveness of our sins and an expression of his
unconditional love for his people.

Faith is basically trust in God. Although faith includes several dimensions or components (knowledge, feeling, voli-
tion), I think trust is the best one-word description of our
response to God's offer of salvation. Faith involves an honest acknowledgment of who we are (including confession
of sin) and an awareness of who God is. I don't mean that
we have to know a lot, but there should be a minimum
awareness of God and ourselves.

The 3 stages of salvation try to encapsule the entire Christian life. Although these stages might be labeled in a variety of ways, one common scheme is conversion, sanctification, and glorification. Conversion is the beginning of salvation. Evangelistic churches place a strong emphasis on
the decision to accept Jesus as Lord and Savior. They highlight testimonies about dramatic conversions such as Paul's

encounter with the risen Jesus on the road to Damascus. This first stage might be called being born again, redeemed, ransomed, justified, or adopted.

The second stage, sanctification, covers the rest of the Christian life up to death. Ideally, a Christian is becoming more holy, mature, "perfect," or a better disciple. My course in ethics covers some issues that turn up here. I would put the emphasis on discipleship here as well. A related emphasis is spirituality. A lot of denominations are encouraging renewed interest in the spiritual disciplines as a way to invigorate the Christian life.

The third stage, glorification, is the culmination or completion of the Christian life. It includes the transition to life in heaven and gaining the resurrected or glorified body described in 1 Corinthians 15.

Well, I could expand on these outlines, but I've gone way beyond 25 words already. But if you only count the key words (grace, faith, conversion, sanctification, glorification), then I did it in 5 words!

A few more quick comments, which may push me past the 25 word limit. First, I think the charismatic movement is one sign that a lot of Christians do not experience the expected growth in their Christian life (sanctification stage). When their life seems dull or routine, the spiritual highs advocated by the charismatics seem very appealing.

Second, the so-called Lordship salvation debate among evangelicals probably reflects the same concern in a different way. The key to that debate seems to be one question: Can someone accept Jesus as Savior without accepting him as Lord? The debate has gone on now through several books. I'm reminded at times of Dietrich Bonhoeffer's concern about cheap grace, or grace without repentance. The concern about discipleship may be my church's way of saying that we expect Christians to mature and act in some distinctive ways.

Third, my scheme reflects a common evangelical understanding of salvation. Obviously denominations that practice infant baptism and confirmation would differ. As part of the "believers church" tradition we disagree with those denominations, although we do not necessarily challenge the authenticity of their salvation experience. The confirmation of teenagers, for example, involves a conscious decision to be a Christian.

Finally, even though I see some scriptural support for the 3 stages scheme, I realize that there are many images or word pictures for salvation in the Bible. I am not sure all of them fit neatly into the temporal scheme. Some terms might be large enough to encompass all of the Christian life. One of my favorite terms, for example, is adoption. God adopts us as his children. Ezekiel used it for God's relation to the Hebrews (Ezek. 16) and Paul notes it as well (Gal. 4:5).

Well, my letter runs on a little, and I need to write some final exams.

From: Chris
To: Dr. Mac
Date: December 27
Subject: Salvation—Reply—Reply

Thanks for the brief(?) overview of the doctrine of salvation. I can see why you will need several Sunday night sessions to cover all of that. Your friends at church might begin to feel like us students: You've told us more than we ever wanted to know on that topic! Seriously, you gave me a lot to think about.

The aspect of salvation I hear the most about is your first stage, conversion. When most of us mention salvation, I think that's all we ever think about. I recall some preacher saying that we do a better job with the prenatal care of Christians than the postnatal care. He meant, I think, that we work hard at evangelism and preparing someone for the initial decision to accept Christ. Sometimes we do not do much to help them grow in the Christian life. One of my seminary classes dwelt on the need for a new members class and the importance of the overall Christian education program of the church, but I hadn't really thought of that as related to the salvation issue.

The thing that has troubled me the most about the salvation issue is the emphasis some preachers make on a "life-changing" experience. One member of my Sunday School class mentioned this recently. He said that he became a Christian very early in life, before he had had the chance to commit a lot of "big" sins. He had "crossed the stream at the narrow point." I think he feels uneasy when preachers stress a dramatic, emotional type of experience, as if that is the only type of valid encounter with God.

Maybe a lot of Christians do have Damascus road experiences. I remember a chapel speaker at college helped me sort this out. He compared the two conversion stories in Acts 16. The more memorable one is the Philippian jailer, who asked the famous question, "What must I do to be saved?" (Acts 16:30). The other conversion, Lydia's, seems quieter, less dramatic (Acts 16:14-15). The speaker emphasized, however, that her experience was just as real as the jailer's.

Although I would like to sit down and talk with you about several of the issues in your last letter, the one that grabbed me the most was your references to "spirituality" and the spiritual disciplines. What kind of activities count as spiritual disciplines? I'm sure Bible study and prayer are basic, but what else would help a Christian grow?

By the way, my family stayed at home this Christmas season. Indeed, I'm writing this e-mail in the middle of a living room that is still very cluttered from unwrapping lots of gifts, especially for the kids. Carolyn and I didn't actually reach a decision about holiday travel. I got "bumped" by senior co-workers, so I had to work. We have a seniority system at the paper, and a couple of other reporters decided to travel over the holidays. Maybe next year we'll discuss the issue again and reach an official family decision.

From: Dr. Mac
To: Chris
Date: January 4
Subject: Spiritual disciplines

I'm glad your family had an enjoyable Christmas, even if your work schedule interfered a little. Our Christmas here was pretty quiet. When my two girls were younger, opening the presents had more suspense to it. Now they get clothes, books, and CDS (music, not money) instead of toys. At least Patty and I don't have to spend Christmas Eve assembling bicycles. Our two dogs have finally gotten over being scared by the tree, gifts, and other seasonal changes in the house.

Oh, I may not have told you that the dog you saw last summer, Barclay, died in the fall. He was named after William Barclay, the New Testament scholar. We had really gotten attached to him, and for a while we were dogless. Eventually we came to our senses and we got two puppies, Hawkeye and Meg. Hawkeye is, of course, named after a character on M*A*S*H, and Meg is named after the friends who gave the puppies to us.

The topic of spiritual disciplines is a very old one, but some Christians are rediscovering some of the old practices. You're right; Bible reading and prayer are good examples of spiritual disciplines. I first got interested in the topic a few years ago when I taught a course on devotional classics from Christian history. One of my seminary profs,

Glenn Hinson, had written a book surveying the literature, *Seekers After Mature Faith*. As I taught that book and read some of the writings he mentioned, I learned a lot about the devotional or spiritual life.

In general the rationale for spiritual exercises parallels that for physical exercises. Our spiritual life should not be flabby. 1 Timothy 4:8 is a good supporting text for both kinds of fitness. Paul encouraged both types of exercise, but he placed the priority on the spiritual. As I've said before, I don't see a radical separation of the two aspects of human nature, physical and spiritual, but I appreciate Paul's emphasis on the relative merit of the two.

One of my favorite authors on this subject is Richard Foster. His book *The Celebration of Discipline* has become a contemporary classic. He mentions a number of traditional spiritual disciplines. A couple of examples will help. First, he encourages fasting. I've kidded my students that I fast between 10:00 pm and 6:00 am, then I break the fast (breakfast!), but I know that is not a sincere fast. Some of my friends think fasting ought to be promoted more in our churches. I also like Foster's emphasis on fasting from things like the television. The principle is that we ought to avoid becoming addicted to anything that will interfere with our relationship to God and others.

Another example is simplicity. Foster developed this concept even more in his book, *The Freedom of Simplicity*. Without proposing a new legalism, he encourages a simple, modest lifestyle that avoids the consumerism that pervades our culture. I realize, of course, that your newspaper needs advertising sales to stay in business, but a lot of those ads seem to be designed to create a "need" for a product rather than provide essential information. Distinguishing real needs from felt needs is crucial to Christian maturity and spiritual fitness.

Well, I'm not suggesting that Foster has all of the answers, but you might look at some of this work for a healthy form of spiritual exercise.

Although I appreciate the renewed emphasis on the spiritual life, I realize that there are some dangers. One danger, for example, is that Christians might start to act like they are holier-than-thou towards Christians who do not practice the same spiritual disciplines with the same rigor. We're supposed to grow and mature in the Christian life, but humility is one characteristic of that maturity. Some people are so proud of their new-found piety that they seem lacking in genuine humility.

I'd better help Patty take our Christmas tree down. Tomorrow I start our January term. I have the usual full house in my ethics course.

From: Chris
To: Dr. Mac

Date: January 11
Subject: Spiritual disciplines—Reply

I found one of the Foster books in our church library. Several people had checked it out over the last couple of years. When I finish it, I may have some more questions. Fasting and simplicity sound a little strange at first glance, but I'm willing to see what he says.

Your short comment about the holier-than-thou criticism really caught my attention. Since Carolyn and I have gotten more active in our church, I've taken some friendly ribbing from some people at work and at church! My co-workers are a little surprised at my recent interest in religious issues. Some of them didn't know much about my background, especially my ministerial training. At church some of my friends kid me about my "worldly" career. I admit I do have to mix and mingle with all types of people as a reporter.

I remember that the word "holy" means being set apart or different. Several times our Sunday School class has discussed what holiness means for us. For example, some of us have struggled with applying holiness to our careers. One fellow told our class that he had changed careers after he became a Christian. I guess withdrawing to a monastery would be the simple way to solve the dilemma. How can Christians be in the world but not of the world? When I was in college I thought the people who lived at the Roman Catholic monastery down the road had taken an extreme approach to the dangers of the "world," but now I see why that option is appealing to some Christians.

Since you're teaching ethics this month, maybe this issue has turned up in class.

From: Dr. Mac
To: Chris
Date: January 18
Subject: Christ and culture

Your last letter raised some fundamental issues for all Christians. I do some lecturing on these issues in my ethics class, but I won't try to give you the whole bit here. Maybe a few comments will help.

Much of what you wrote relates to the "Christ and Culture" issue. How do Christians relate to the world in which they live? H. Richard Niebuhr's classic study on *Christ and Culture* is still a valuable overview of the issues.

One quick example of the possible tension between Christ and culture would be how churches respond to Super Bowl Sunday. Some churches alter their evening schedule to allow their members to watch the game. Other churches keep to business as usual, making no changes at all in their schedule. By the way, you can tell that I am defining "culture"

very broadly, including classical music (high-brow culture) and sports (popular culture or low-brow culture).

Christians across the centuries have adopted several basic stances on the Christ and culture issue. The monks at
the monastery in our town have adopted one of the classic responses. Some people think that our denomination's
response to culture is similar since some of our ances-
tors withdrew from mainstream culture. I suspect that
they were forced to take that stance in order to survive,
not just make a moral statement. In recent years some
Christians seem to have adopted a close alliance with
our culture in North America. As you might guess, the
issues can get very complex, and I would have to sketch
out a lot of biblical, historical, and theological material
to show you why I don't like either extreme, withdrawal
or identification.

I do believe that Christians should develop a distinctive
lifestyle, one that may often be in tension with our culture. Foster's emphasis on simplicity is a good example
of the direction I would go. I don't feel compelled to take
the vow of poverty like the monks, but a vow of simplicity is very appealing to me.

Perhaps a handy label for a healthy Christian relation to
our culture would be "incarnational." Just as Jesus min-
istered by interacting with those who needed his help,
so we should discover ways to be redemptive in our culture. If we withdraw from culture, we've lost our chance

to have any impact on it. If we adopt cultural values completely, we can't be salt and light (Matthew 5:13-16).

One way to get a handle on the holiness issue is to look at some of the key texts in the Bible. One of my favorites is Leviticus 19, part of the so-called Holiness Code. One of the basic themes there is the imitation of God. Since God is holy, his people should be holy. Of course, this imitation theme fits other divine attributes as well. Also, that chapter gives lots of illustrations of holiness in action. Holiness affects all of life, including how we harvest our crops (vv. 9-10), treat the handicapped (v. 14), and the elderly (v. 32).

One of my classroom examples of the difficulty of holiness involves that ice cream store I can see from my office window. As long as I avoid gluttony, there is no sin in patronizing it. If, however, that store were part of a larger corporation that produced a product I thought was sinful (pornography, for instance), could I still buy ice cream there? One of my students thought that question was silly, but someone trying to be totally untainted by the world would worry about it. Would buying that ice cream somehow mean I condoned everything that corporation did? Would I need to practice an economic boycott of the ice cream store in order to protest another division of the corporation making X-rated films? I guess my point is that, although I advocate holiness for Christians, making some decisions can be very complex.

Well, I promised I wouldn't give you the whole lecture. In case you want to do some reading beyond Foster, Niebuhr's *Christ and Culture* is a classic review of the historic positions held by Christians, and several books by John Howard Yoder, such as *The Politics of Jesus*, would give you a strong statement about keeping some distance between Chris and culture.

By the way, the conference basketball season has just started. As usual, we need to win all of our home games and try to get a few road wins in order to have a chance at the regular season championship! Being ranked high in the national polls would help our chances of getting to the national tournament in March.

Of course, most of my students are more interested in the Super Bowl right now. Maybe I need to remind them of the *Sports Illustrated* article "Does God Care Who Wins the Super Bowl?" The writer did a good job of interviewing athletes and theologians on that topic. Many of the NFL players thought God did care about the game, but most of the theologians disagreed.

10

Who Needs the Church?

From: Chris
To: Dr. Mac
Date: January 26
Subject: Family life center

Thanks for your last e-mail. I'll try to follow up on some of the books you mentioned, even though I don't get much reading done any more. I usually carry a paperback with me so I can read during my loose change time, such as when I'm waiting on people I need to interview. I used to read some at night, but it's amazing how tired I am after helping Carolyn get the kids cleaned up and ready for bed.

I've mentioned in recent letters that Carolyn and I have been pretty active in our church lately. Since you mentioned a debate at your church's business meeting, I thought you might be interested in a discussion we had recently at our church. Our Long Range Planning Committee had met for about a year, trying to develop a comprehensive plan for the next 5 to 10 years. Since there had been a series of public discussions, most of the recommendations were predictable. The one that received the most discussion was about building a "family life center." Although the majority of our people seemed open to the idea, a few were very upset. They thought that we ought to keep our emphasis on evangelism and missions. Building a gymnasium did not seem that evangelistic to them. Anyway, the committee offered to have another public hearing on that proposal and bring it back to the church at the next business meeting.

Although I didn't really have any strong feelings on the issue, the heated discussion reminded me of why Carolyn and I had sort of dropped out of church life for a while. We had felt that churches were too institutional or bureaucratic. Programs had become more important than people. Business meetings dwelt on issues that didn't seem that important to me as a young husband and father.

Even though we have found the last few months very meaningful, especially our couples Sunday School class, that business meeting was kind of a downer.

Well, I trust your spring semester has got started well. I would be interested in what you think about a church having a family life center.

From: Dr. Mac
To: Chris

Date: February 4
Subject: Family life center—Reply

Our second semester is going well so far. Unfortunately, I need to start writing exams already.

I understand your reaction to the debate at the church business meeting. Even though I get bored at times in those meetings, I realize they are important. Sometimes you can see where a church's real priorities are in those meetings, especially if the decisions relate to money! When, for instance, a church votes on its annual budget, it is making a theological statement about what really matters to the congregation. Your church's decision for or against a family life center will likewise express its understanding of the nature and purpose of the church.

Since my church has not discussed the issue, I don't know what we would do. A key issue for your church will be how a family life center will help it fulfill its overall goals. Let me mention a couple of possibilities. On one hand, you could argue that a family life center would help the fellowship of the church. A lot of activities could be planned (including basketball, racquetball, skating, and crafts) that would enrich the life of the congregation. With a well-planned program, all age groups could be involved. With the fragmentation of the family being lamented by a lot of church leaders, a family life center might be very useful as a place where all members of a family could relax and play.

On the other hand, the family life center might be helpful in outreach to the community. Unless there is a YMCA or similar facility near your church, your recreational activities might attract some people who would not initially be interested in Bible study or worship services. As your church cultivates a relationship with these people, they might be drawn more and more into the life of the church. A family life center could be an effective evangelistic tool, at least in an indirect way.

I presume your church's long-range planning committee proposed the family life center for one or both of these reasons, fellowship and outreach. Since our college has a program in church recreation, I'm probably biased here. Christians should be concerned about physical fitness. Our word "gymnasium" is based on Greek; Paul used it in 1 Timothy 4:8 when he said physical training is good! Years ago, I reminded our college's athletic director that the root word for gymnasium means "naked," but I didn't recommend that our physical education program follow a literal application; of course, they could save some money by not buying uniforms for the athletic teams. So you see why knowing a little Greek is dangerous for me!

Let me know what your church decides to do about the family life center.

The basketball teams are doing well. The women's team is ranked 5th nationally, and the men's team is ranked 16th. Maybe both teams will make the playoffs.

From: Chris
To: Dr. Mac
Date: February 12
Subject: Worship committee

I'll let you know what our church votes to do about the family life center. I'd forgotten about the original meaning of "gymnasium"; perhaps that's why "family life center" became a popular alternative term.

Our Long-Range Planning Committee had developed a list of tasks for our church, and the proposal to build a family life center was based on both outreach and fellowship. The other tasks were worship, social concern, and education. Although they did not rank those tasks, they tried to correlate each recommendation to at least one of the tasks.

One other recommendation was that a Worship Committee be appointed to advise the church staff on the quality of our worship services. Carolyn was invited to be on the committee to represent the young adult age group. Each quarter they are to evaluate the main worship services and make suggestions for improvement. Normally our pastor and the minister of music work together to plan our worship services. No one's been upset about our worship, but there was no formal means for input from the lay people on the worship. Our worship leaders have been very supportive of the recommendation, but Carolyn has been a little nervous. She realizes that some people have very strong opinions about the worship service, including the type of music and the length of sermons.

Since you do some supply preaching, I guess you have seen all types of worship services. When I was a ministerial student in college, I preached in a few of the smaller churches in our area. Sometimes it was a real adventure seeing how each congregation worshiped.

I was glad to hear about the basketball teams doing well. I've never done any sports reporting for our paper, but I check a lot of the scores as they come in.

From: Dr. Mac
To: Chris
Date: February 19
Subject: Worship committee—Reply

I'm delighted that Carolyn was appointed to be on the new Worship Committee. I can appreciate her uneasiness; it is easy to step on toes. I remember when one pastor wanted to put the collection of offerings at the end of the order of worship. Some people were really upset, as if taking the offering right before the sermon was part of some divine plan.

The list of tasks developed by your Long-Range Planning Committee seems very comprehensive. If they had tried to rank them in order of importance, they might have had some serious disagreement. Some people, for example, argue that worship is the primary task. If we meet God in a meaningful way in our public worship, they insist, then we will be motivated to do things such as education, evangelism, and social ministry. Other Christians would insist that evangelism or missions should be the highest priority for the local church.

One of my concerns in recent years has been that some worship services have taken a turn towards entertainment. If I were a pastor again, I suppose I would really struggle with how to inspire or challenge the people without resorting to the sensational. For instance, some people seem to have such short attention spans that they need something dramatic or spectacular to happen often.

As Carolyn's committee begins their work, they will probably have to develop a set of criteria for evaluating the current worship services. One way to approach that task is to itemize the essential components of worship. Christians often include adoration or praise, thanksgiving, confession of sins, and commitment to service. Each worship activity (such as congregational hymns, anthems, scripture reading, prayers, sermons, offering) could be assessed in light of how well it highlights one or more of these components.

Since I do preach in some churches in this area, I've noticed that many are very strong in areas such as praise and commitment to service. Many churches are weak, however, in confession of sins and assurance of forgiveness. Often all I hear about this area is a brief, almost perfunctory, reference to sins in a prayer.

Recently I've done some reading on the relation of worship to character development. A textbook I used in my Contemporary Theology course stressed that one result of genuine worship is the improvement of the character of the worshiper. William Willimon's *The Service of God*, my text, insisted that my basic identity as a Christian, including my character and my virtues, is shaped by regular experiences in public worship. Another writer put it crisply, "liturgy shapes lifestyle." Of course, I've been impressed for a long time with the power of music. I suspect most Christians learn more theology through hymns than through many sermons.

Although I resonate with this emphasis on the transformation or development of character through worship, I see at least one danger. The primary purpose of worship is to acknowledge the worth of God. Our improvement may be an important by-product of that worship experience, but we should avoid distorting worship by making it human-centered. The intrinsic purpose of worship is the glorification of God. An instrumental purpose, improving the worshiper, needs to be secondary, lest we take our eyes off of God.

One of my favorite illustrations of the nature of worship comes from Soren Kierkegaard's book, *Purity of Heart Is

to Will One Thing*. There he compares worship to attending the theater. The enclosed chart adapts his illustration:

Enclosure:

	Ordinary Worship	Real Worship
Actor:	Preacher	Congregation
Audience:	Congregation	God
Prompter:	God	Preacher

I hope I've done justice to Kierkegaard! He insists that the
congregation should be active in worship, with the worship leaders prompting them to worship God correctly. The
real audience is God himself. Unfortunately, many of our
churches have made the worship leader the "star" of the
play, and the worshipers are very passive spectators of what
happens on stage. If Carolyn's worship committee can find
an effective way to implement Kierkegaard's insights, they
could patent it and make a mint!

Well, you can tell this is a subject I like to talk about. Don't
feel like I'm making a lot of suggestions for the committee.
The best decisions, the ones most fitting for your church,
need to emerge from the dialogue among the committee
members.

From: Chris
To: Dr. Mac
Date: February 26
Subject: Lent

As usual, I shared your e-mail with Carolyn. I'm sure she will keep some of your ideas in mind when the committee meets. We both have enjoyed the worship services at our church, and Carolyn did not intend to recommend any major changes. Your example from Kierkegaard, however, was new to us, and we realized that we have been "spectators" rather than active participants a lot of times. Of course, now that Kevin attends "big church" with us, we can't be too apathetic.

My ignorance of the theology of worship (would that be the right label?) may be typical of many church members. I attend worship regularly, but I don't usually try to figure out why I do what. I was reminded of my ignorance recently at a coffee break at work. Some of my co-workers are active in other denominations, and they mentioned Ash Wednesday and Lent. I had a vague knowledge of these terms, but I was a little confused. When I got home, I looked those events up in a reference book. Lent is the season from Ash Wednesday up to Easter Sunday. My co-workers had attended an Ash Wednesday service recently. Apparently their church stresses the need for confession and repentance in this season. I suppose if I had taken more church history in college or seminary I would have known more about these traditions.

Why does our denomination ignore these seasons? I've noticed that some of our churches have started mentioning Advent as the preparation for Christmas. Our church has had an Advent wreath in the sanctuary the last few years, but nothing has been said about Lent.

From: Dr. Mac
To: Chris
Date: March 3
Subject: Lent—Reply

Don't feel too guilty about your ignorance of Lent. I'm not sure of all the reasons why most Baptists have ignored Lent. Perhaps they think of Lent as a Catholic ceremony. Since the crucifixion and resurrection of Jesus are central to our faith, we ought to prepare for Easter with real care. Maybe if the celebration of Advent becomes meaningful to a lot of your church members, you might want to look at planning a series or services leading up to Easter. Whether or not you ever call it "Lent," the idea of preparing for a special event would be helpful. Occasionally I am asked to speak in churches outside our denomination. Recently I participated in some lenten services in a Presbyterian church. The services were very meaningful to me because they helped me focus my attention on the meaning of Easter for several weeks rather than just the one Sunday.

Courses on church history or worship might have acquainted you with the Christian year (events such as Advent, Lent, and Pentecost). The early church developed these events in order to provide a systematic, comprehensive celebration of the main themes of our faith. Of course, the birth, life, death, and resurrection of Jesus provide the core of the Christian year.

Pentecost reminds us of the gift of the Holy Spirit in Acts 2. If a church had a regular observance of this date in the Christian year, maybe there would be more consistent preaching and teaching on the Holy Spirit.

Preachers who follow the Christian calendar normally use a lectionary to guide their preaching. The lectionary lists relevant scripture passages for each Sunday. Ministers develop their sermons from those texts. Most of my students think that using a lectionary to guide the selection of their sermon texts would hinder their spontaneity, but a few former students and ministers I know appreciate the discipline of that system. Following a lectionary would keep a minister from riding his favorite hobby horse every Sunday. An extra benefit from a lectionary is that several Bible texts are usually read during the service. Some of our churches read or hear only the sermon text. I wish we would do more public reading of the Bible.

By the way, I'm curious if Carolyn's worship committee will look at worship activities such as funerals and weddings. Those can be very meaningful events. You can probably remember your wedding very well. In addition to the Christian calendar, there are some traditional worship services that highlight our human developmental cycle, what I heard called the "womb to tomb" cycle. My church, for example, has a baby dedication ceremony each spring. The parents and the church dedicate themselves to the nurture of the babies.

I wish I had the creativity to develop a worship service for teenagers when they get their driver's license. That may be the biggest personal or social event for a teenager, but it seems the church ignores it. Maybe some recognition is made in the youth Sunday School department.

By the way, has your church decided what to do about the family life center?

From: Chris
To: Dr. Mac
Date: March 9
Subject: Women pastors

Our church voted at the last business meeting to approve the recommendation that we build a family life center. A few people voted against the recommendation, but the vast majority thought the family life center could provide a real ministry to our congregation as well to the community. Some people were afraid that the family life center would be open to church members only, but the Long Range Planning Committee was very clear that it should be open to the community as well. One committee member recalled a slogan our church had used many years ago, "Journey inward, journey outward." She said that our congregation tried to balance activities that edified our members and developed fellowship alongside activities that reached out to the larger community. If we had the journey inward only, she said, we might become a religious clique. If we had the journey outward alone, then we might neglect the "spiritual disciplines"! Anyway, now the church has to raise some money and hire an architect.

Besides that update, I thought you might be interested in a newspaper assignment I got recently. My editor asked me to interview the new pastor of a church in our town. The regular religion editor is in the hospital, and the editor was impressed with my interview of the minister who has visions. Anyway, the new pastor is a woman! She's married, has 1 child, and had been associate pastor at a large Methodist church before she was appointed to this parish.

After I wrote my article, I talked to my pastor to see what he thought about a woman being a pastor. He was pretty cautious and insisted that he not be quoted in the newspaper. Although he was not dogmatic, he seemed to think that many Baptists would be very reluctant to accept a woman as the senior pastor of a church.

I know you have done some teaching and research in the area of feminist theology and the biblical view of women. Off the record (!), what do you think about women being ordained for the ministry? I remember some heated discussions at seminary about the issue, but I hadn't really thought about it much until I interviewed the new pastor.

From: Dr. Mac
To: Chris
Date: March 16
Subject: Women pastors—Reply

Your question about the ordination of women is still a hot issue in our denomination. I have done some reading in feminist theology, but I'm far from an expert on the subject. Several years ago I taught a January course here on "Women and the Bible," but I haven't made that topic a focus for serious research.

Reluctantly, I'll try to make a few comments on this hot topic. For the sake of simplicity, let me divide your question about women pastors into two parts. First, what about women in the ministry? Second, should women be ordained? Although they are related issues, they might be easier to handle one at a time.

First, the question of women in the ministry. Sincere, well-meaning Christians have argued different positions on this. Certainly I am not a crusader, but I try to be open to what the Bible says on any subject. Most interpreters cite the passages that deal directly with the role of women in the

church, but, as usual, I think we need to keep a larger context in mind as well. There are at least 2 types of relevant
passages. One type would be the general texts about the
status of women. For example, Genesis 1 tells us that both
male and female were created in the image of God.
Galatians 3:28 says that in Christ there is neither male nor
female. The other type of passage deals directly with
women in the church. (Other texts deal with women in the
home and women in society in general.) In 1 Timothy, for
example, Paul says women should not teach or have authority over men (2:12) and that pastors (bishops) should
be the husband of one wife (3:2).

As you would guess, there are many different views on
each of these texts. At the risk of oversimplification, an oc-
cupational hazard for me, I'll mention a few different per-
spectives. Some argue, for example, that Galatians 3:28 has
a spiritual application only; women, like men, can be saved.
In other words, God is an equal opportunity savior. Others
insist that the text also has a social application. In other
words, in Christ all old distinctions (Jew/Greek, slave/free,
male/female) are obsolete in the sense of superiority and
inferiority. Feminist theologians, of course, follow that second view and insist that leadership positions should be
open to women. They compare the emancipation of women
to the abolition of slavery.

The 1 Timothy texts have also elicited conflicting opinions.
Do women have the right to speak in church? Although
the passage seems very clear, some ask if the issue is really

about gender. In the first century women were not trained in theology or scripture. Maybe, say feminists, the real issue is experience or training, not gender. Earlier in that chapter, they note, Paul outlawed gold jewelry and fancy hairdos for Christian women. Churches that reject women ministers often ignore that passage or say it is culturally conditioned. Feminists argue that Paul had to make some accommodations to his day, but his main teaching is clear in Galatians 3:28.

Likewise, the husband of one wife concept becomes ambiguous for some. Paul may have meant that all pastors had to be married men, but that would eliminate single male pastors as well as female ministers. Some argue that the real issue is marital fidelity or a critique of polygamy. Well, if you read 10 commentaries, you may get 10 or more opinions!

I think the issue of women in ministry is more complex than some people realize. My bottom line response is that one cannot be dogmatic. If a women believes God has called her into the ministry, my job is not to reject her call. As a teacher I try to help all of my students clarify their call and act on their interpretation of that experience. When you first wrote to me last year, I suggested that you need to clarify if you were indeed called to ministry. If so, then there are some more decisions you need to make (continue seminary? what kind of ministry?). I would try to ask the same questions of a female ministerial student.

The second issue was about the ordination of women. I separated the two issues because I know of some women ministers who have not requested ordination. Perhaps they are reluctant to create a controversy, or maybe they feel they can be effective ministers without a seal of approval.

The underlying question here is "Why do we ordain anyone?" The biblical evidence is pretty slim on the theology and practice of ordination. Most of what we do today, outside of the laying on of hands, is based on tradition or custom. Although I think an ordination service can be very meaningful, many of our people are not very clear on what that exact meaning is. For example, many churches have commissioning services for youth groups going out on mission trips. What is the difference between a commissioning and an ordination? Most of my students see a time distinction. Commissioning is for a definite task for a short time (2-week mission trip to Mexico). Ordination is for life. Our mission board, however, commissions career missionaries for life.

I ordinarily don't want a government agency settling theological issues, but I read somewhere that missionaries (male and female) are considered ordained by the Internal Revenue Service. In that case, our denomination has ordained thousands of women ministers (missionaries)!

Ordination, simply stated, is the time when a church says "Amen" to a minister's calling. The real initiative is God's; he calls the minister. The church's responsibility is to give a public affirmation ("so be it") to that calling. By custom, some churches give ordained ministers certain privileges or responsibilities, but ordination does not confer any magical powers upon the candidate.

To get back to your original question, I suppose I'm giving you one of those frustrating, evasive answers, a "definite maybe." If God has called a woman into the ministry, then her responsibility is to accept that call. A church's responsibility and privilege is to ordain her and let her exercise her gifts and talents in that congregation.

My comments are officially "off the record," but I certainly address these issues in class and in churches. The problem is that many people want very simple answers to complex issues. If you want to do some reading and quote some scholars, there has been a flood of books and journal articles. A helpful book by evangelicals that leans towards the feminist side is *Women, Authority and the Bible,* edited by Alvera Mickelsen. A collection of papers and responses from a conference, this volume provides a good introduction to the issues, even if you don't agree with their conclusions.

By the way, I'm glad you get to write on religious issues occasionally.

A quick update on the basketball teams. Both teams did well in the conference tournaments last week. The women won their tournament, and the men finished second. Both teams are still ranked nationally, so they will be in the national tournaments.

From: Chris
To: Dr. Mac
Date: March 25
Subject: Off the record

I'll keep my part of the bargain and let your last letter be off the record. Some of what you said was similar to my pastor's comments. He was a little less open to the possibility of a woman pastor, but he mentioned some of the same Bible passages. I couldn't find the book you mentioned locally, but I was impressed with some other recent books on the subject in our church library.

Have you seen *Women in the Church* by Stan Grenz and Denise Kjesbo? I've read a little in it, and it seems like a good overview of the issues. Their book reminded me of the many women who held leadership positions in biblical times. I was familiar with the female judge, Deborah, but I had forgotten about the female prophets, such as Huldah. If a women could proclaim God's message in a patriarchal society, maybe a woman could preach today.

When I mentioned to my editor that I had talked to my pastor and written to you, he suggested I consider doing a follow-up article on the status of women in the ministry. If I find the time to do some research, I'll try to compare the views of several denominations. If I need some good, short quotes, I may give you a call.

By the way, I'm still puzzled about how to interpret my "call" to the ministry. Our correspondence has been very enjoyable, but I don't know that I need to be a professional minister. My reporting work is very satisfying to me.

Thanks for the news about the basketball teams. Our paper focuses so much on the "big" schools (NCAA) that sometimes I have to ask the sports editor for the small school scores.

From: Dr. Mac
To: Chris
Date: March 29
Subject: Off the record—Reply

I'm glad you found the book by Grenz and Kjesbo. I'm familiar with much of Grenz's writings, but that book was new to me. I hope you are able to follow up on the women in ministry issue for your newspaper. I've told several classes that this issue is one of the biggest ones for Christians to confront today.

Well, the national basketball tournaments are over. The good news is that the women won the championship. The men lost in the semi-finals in a heart-breaker. My students are really excited! It will be very difficult for any serious learning to occur for a while.

11

Where Are You Going?

From: Dr. Mac
To: Chris
Date: April 3
Subject: Emergency call

I hope our phone conversation this morning helped a little. When you called, I thought you might be following up on our correspondence about women in the ministry. I'm really sorry about the accident and the death of Kevin's friend. It's very hard for me to imagine what I would feel if one of my girls died. Somehow the death of a small child is especially difficult, both for the parents, for other children in the family, and for the child's friends.

Although I did not have any simple suggestions for you, I know you and Carolyn will be very compassionate in ministering to the Ketchums. David's sudden death must be overwhelming to them. They may still be in a state of shock now, but the reality of the situation will set in soon enough.

When I was in seminary, my pastor's daughter died of leukemia. The entire church empathized with that family, and the pastor was very candid in his sermons about his emotional and spiritual ups and downs. Those sermons were later published and have helped other parents deal with their grief over the loss of a child. You might want to read the book or get a copy for the Ketchums to read eventually. It's *Tracks of a Fellow Struggler* by John Claypool.

I'm glad the Ketchums asked you to participate in the funeral for David. I don't know if you ever led in a funeral service while you were in school, but even the few comments you make, along with your pastor's sermon, can be very helpful in the grieving process.

From: Chris
To: Dr. Mac
Date: April 10
Subject: 3 views of death

The last week and a half have been very agonizing for us and the Ketchums. Thanks again for reassuring me on the phone and in your last e-mail. Some of the people in our Sunday School class know I attended seminary and really thought I ought to have all of the answers when David died. The Ketchums are some of our best friends, and I wanted to touch base with you about how to minister to them. The funeral service went as well as could be expected. Carolyn and I are going to take the Ketchums out to eat tomorrow night. We don't want to hover over them or invade their private grief, but they seemed to welcome the chance to talk to us again.

I think our Easter service yesterday had a real note of urgency, since everyone knew about David's funeral on Thursday. My pastor usually does a fine job in the sermon, but I thought he outdid himself yesterday. His sermon was on a Christian view of death. I don't recall hearing a sermon on that topic, except at funerals. I don't usually take notes on sermons, but this time I jotted down my pastor's main points. When I talked to him after the service, he said he borrowed some of his outline from a theologian's discussion in a textbook!

My pastor stressed that death is portrayed in three main ways in the Bible. First, death is destruction. I'm sure the Ketchums could identify with this point especially. The death of a close friend or family member is often experienced as a loss. The sudden death of a young child seems especially tragic. Second, death is departure. Our pastor referred to Paul's comments as he anticipated his own death:

"For I am already being poured out like a drink offering, and the time has come for my departure. I have fought the good fight, I have finished the race, I have kept the faith." (2 Tim. 4:6-7 NIV)

Death is the transition from this life to a new life with God.

Third, death is dead. He stressed that Jesus' death and resurrection had defeated death. Christians will die physically, but they can experience eternal life now and in the future. His reference here was 2 Timothy 1:10.

David's death has caused me to do a lot of thinking about eschatology. When we studied the doctrine of "last things" in your class, I really wasn't too interested in the topic. I had always thought of issues such as heaven and hell as a kind of pie-in-the-sky escapism. As I've thought about this freak accident, I've realized that those doctrines are very important to grieving people.

Thanks again for your help in recent days.

From: Dr. Mac
To: Chris
Date: April 16
Subject: 3 views of death—Reply

Your comment about the relevance of eschatology is probably typical of my current students as well. Although there is some curiosity about the details of eschatology, college students in their early 20s often assume these topics are too theoretical to be of value to them. The students who have had family members die are more involved in the discussion. Occasionally I'll have a ministerial student ask me for advice as he prepares to do a funeral sermon. The only other topic that seems to evoke much curiosity or discussion is out-of-body or near-death experiences.

Your pastor's outline gives a good, balanced portrayal of the biblical view of death. Maybe I should add it to my notes on eschatology. I especially like the way he balanced the positive and negative aspects of death. Many, many people see death only as the enemy. Of course, Paul used that imagery in a famous text. Death is the last enemy (1 Cor. 15:26). I suspect that the development of some medical technology is guided by the conviction that death is always to be challenged and defeated. As much as I appreciate the benefits of medicine, I'm not sure that death is always the enemy.

The notion that death can be a friend as well as a foe is also biblical. Your pastor's emphasis on death as departure fits here. I also like Paul's admission in Philippians 1:21-26 that he preferred to die and be with Christ. I've worked with enough older people with serious illnesses to realize that many people reach a point when they are ready to die. When I was in seminary I chatted with an older man in a hospital. When he told me he wanted to die, I naively tried to convince him that he should want to live. Very gently he chastised me, "Young man, when you are as old as I am and as sick as I am, you'll want to die, too."

In my ethics class we deal with a number of life and death issues. I encourage my students to develop their view of death as the context for looking at specific issues such as euthanasia, living wills, and physician-assisted suicide. These issues are very complex, but a Christian view of death is an essential element in the decision-making process.

By the way, how is Kevin reacting to his friend's death? Many young children first encounter death through the loss of a pet or the death of grandparents. I'm sure you and Carolyn will be sensitive to his grief. Since he was at the same birthday party when the accident occurred, he will likely have very vivid memories of the event.

On a much lighter note, my semester is going pretty well. The stretch from spring break to final exams seems very long, especially for the seniors looking forward to graduation. "Senioritis" is still a common malady here, although it is probably only an intense form of spring fever.

From: Chris
To: Dr. Mac
Date: April 23
Subject: Intermediate state

I had forgotten about "senioritis"! I had a really bad case the spring of my senior year. I thought I had saved some easier courses for that last semester, but your theology class was harder than I expected.

Kevin is doing pretty well. Like most pre-schoolers, he has a hard time understanding death and afterlife. Carolyn and I have tried to answer some of his questions, but explaining heaven is hard with a 4-year-old. When he asked where David was now, we assured him David was with Jesus. I knew there was no simple way to explain the intermediate state! I recall your presentation on the many different views of what happens between physical death and our final destiny (limbo, purgatory, paradise, heaven, reincarnation). When Kevin asked me if David could see what we are doing "down here," I was really stuck for a simple answer.

The Ketchums are still very distraught, but they keep attending church. Our Sunday School class has really pulled together to support them, and they have also found a support group in our town for parents who have lost children.

I happened to mention David's death to some of my co-workers at a company cookout recently. We had a very interesting discussion about death and afterlife. Normally we discuss sports and TV shows, but the discussion was a lot more serious this time. Even the people who don't attend church got involved. Almost everyone believed in some form of afterlife, but we disagreed on what it was like. Of course, some recent movies about afterlife fueled the discussion more than anything else.

One of the biggest discussions was about heaven and hell. I know that most Christians believe in two possible eternal states, heaven and hell, but some of the other newspaper people weren't so sure that those were the only options. One or two even said reincarnation might make sense.

Well, I need to get back to work. My latest big assignment is to interview some of the city commissioners about a proposed tax increase.

From: Dr. Mac
To: Chris
Date: April 29
Subject: Intermediate state—Reply

Your company cookout was an unusual setting for a theology discussion, especially about eschatology, but I think most people are curious about death and afterlife. Popular movies about these issues, such as "Ghost" or "Always" a few years ago, can stimulate some interesting discussion. I can usually count on my students having seen those shows, even when they don't have time to study. The sci-fi movie "Contact" was not primarily about end times, but it prompted some questions about contact with the dead from a few of my students.

Although there are numerous possible scenarios for afterlife, most views can be clustered under two headings: single destiny or double destiny. The single destiny view insists that all people have a common end. Some argue that we die and there is no afterlife. The Epicureans in ancient times held that view, and Ecclesiastes 3:20-22 raises some interesting questions about afterlife. According to most of the surveys I've seen in recent years, most Americans seem to believe in some type of afterlife. Others who hold to a single destiny view argue that everyone will eventually make it to heaven. Known as universalism, this view seems very popular when people highlight the love of God. Some Christians have been universalists, but universalism has been considered a heresy by most denominations.

The double destiny view has been the traditional one for most Christians. Christians generally affirm that some go to heaven and others to hell. As you know, there are lots of disagreements about how to interpret the Bible on these destinies. For example, is heaven a place (literal interpretation) or a condition (figurative)? Some older people, widowed and remarried, are concerned about the issue of which spouse they will be with in heaven. I've been asked by some older people about whose "mansion" they will go to when they die (see John 14:2 in King James).

Some people believe in a double destiny but deny the existence of hell. They argue that the saved join God in heaven, but the lost simply cease to exist. Known as annihilationism or conditional immortality, this view has even been advocated by some evangelicals.

We don't hear much preaching on heaven and hell anymore, but I think there is a natural curiosity about these topics. One of my favorite books on this topic is *The Great Divorce* by C. S. Lewis. Lewis describes an imaginary bus ride from hell to heaven. Although I don't agree with everything he proposes, I like the notion that some people choose not to serve God and, in effect, choose hell as their destiny:

"There are only two kinds of people in the end: those who say to God, 'Thy will be done,' and those to whom God says, in the end, 'Thy will be done.' All that are in Hell, choose it. Without that self-choice there could be no Hell."

Although I have no inside information, beyond the witness of scripture, I believe the double destiny view is correct.

I see the need to deal with sincere questions about eschatology, but I try to stay away from too much speculation. For instance, I heard once that everyone in heaven will be 33 years old, since that is the age Jesus died! Why these views ever get advocated boggles my mind. Anyway, I hope you stick to more relevant issues. Of course, talking to a child about death and afterlife makes avoiding speculation difficult. For instance, I don't know for sure how to answer Kevin's question about whether his dead friend knows what's happening on earth. The comic strip "Family Circus" often has a dead grandparent watching his family. Sometimes I think that the "cloud of witnesses" in Hebrews 12:2 might include departed loved ones.

The type of biblical literature that deals the most with eschatology is apocalyptic. My working definition for this kind of literature is "the symbolic description of the end of an era." When I'm tempted to get bogged down in the details of the symbolism, I try to remember that the original author intended a comforting message for suffering people. I doubt if the biblical writer intended for us to develop elaborate timetables. For example, the famous "rapture" passage in 1 Thessalonians even concludes with Paul stressing the pastoral, practical nature of the subject: "Therefore encourage each other with these words" (4:18 NIV).

Well, enough about afterlife. I need to devote some time to class preparation and this life for now. Keep in touch.

From: Chris
To: Dr. Mac
Date: May 7
Subject: Service or speculation

Thanks for your last e-mail. I especially liked your comment about avoiding too much speculation about eschatology. I think I've done a pretty good job of balancing a cautious interest in eschatology with some other priorities. I realize now that not all eschatological discussions are escapist, but I see so many problems in our world today that I think Christians ought to devote more energy to solving them.

Several years ago I read Calvin Miller's book, *The Philippian Fragment.* That imaginary correspondence about the early church in Philippi makes many serious points through humor. I especially like the story about Phoebe and the women's scroll study. One day the group debated whether Jesus would return before or after the great tribulation. The vote was a tie, and Phoebe was puzzled how to vote. Eventually she decided to help the lepers rather than worry about the details of Jesus' return. There were no endtime charts in the leper colony!

I don't think Miller means to dismiss all discussion of Jesus' return, but his emphasis on service rather than speculative debate struck a responsive chord with me. Perhaps the old saying, "First things first," fits here. As long as Christians affirm some of the basic truths, such as the return of Christ, judgment, heaven and hell, I'm not sure the details are worth the debate. I hope I'm not avoiding issues like the millennium or the tribulation because I'm lazy. My pastor doesn't say much about these issues in sermons, but he does preach on the larger eschatological issues, such as death and afterlife, the return of Jesus, and Christian hope.

By the way, I had not heard about the theory that everyone in heaven is 33. I supposed we would be the same age we were when we died, but that is pure speculation!

From: Dr. Mac
To: Chris
Date: May 15
Subject: Millennium

Your story from Calvin Miller's book was delightful. I've enjoyed everything I've read of his, but he is so prolific that I've missed some of his works. I found the book in a used book store I frequent and am about half way through it. His use of humor is outstanding.

"First things first" has been my basic approach to eschatology as well. Students are often curious about where I land on some of the more controversial issues, but I am personally satisfied with a pretty basic set of beliefs.

A couple of days ago I covered the millennial schemes in class. As usual, some were very interested, but most saw these as non-issues. When I came to college, I had been immersed in one millennial system. I was very surprised to learn that some Christians actually had different views from what I knew. Later, I recall being very impressed when a famous pastor wrote that he had changed his mind on the millennium. Whether or not his new position is better, I appreciated his candor, as a mid-career minister, in publicly announcing his shift. Some people seem to be reluctant to admit such changes.

If I were a pastor, I wouldn't see the need to treat the details of those systems, but I would stress eschatology occasionally. If eschatology is totally ignored, then misunder-standings or even false teachings crop up. Some of these issues might be better handled in a teaching format. My pastor has recently led a series of discussions on the book of Revelation on Sunday evenings. There was a lively give and take, and most of the major options were mentioned.

Since my pastor had to be out of town one Sunday, he asked me to cover the millennium issue. I kidded him about the convenient scheduling, but I was glad to do it. The 3 major views are premillennialism, postmillennialism, and amillennialism. Postmillennialism says that Jesus will come back at the end of a long period of peace and prosperity. That view has some adherents today, but it was more popular at the end of the 19th century when our culture was more optimistic about the future. Amillennialism rejects a literal 1000 year reign of Christ but affirms a spiritual reign in believers' lives today.

Premillennialism has been very popular in many evangeli-cal denominations. Basically it says Jesus will come back before the millennium. Some of the strongest debate is be-tween two versions of this view. Historic premillennialists generally are less literalistic and affirm one basic return of Jesus. Dispensational premillennialists are literalistic and talk about two separate returns of Christ. The enclosed charts, although oversimplified, might help remind you of these views.

Enclosure:

Historic Premillennialist

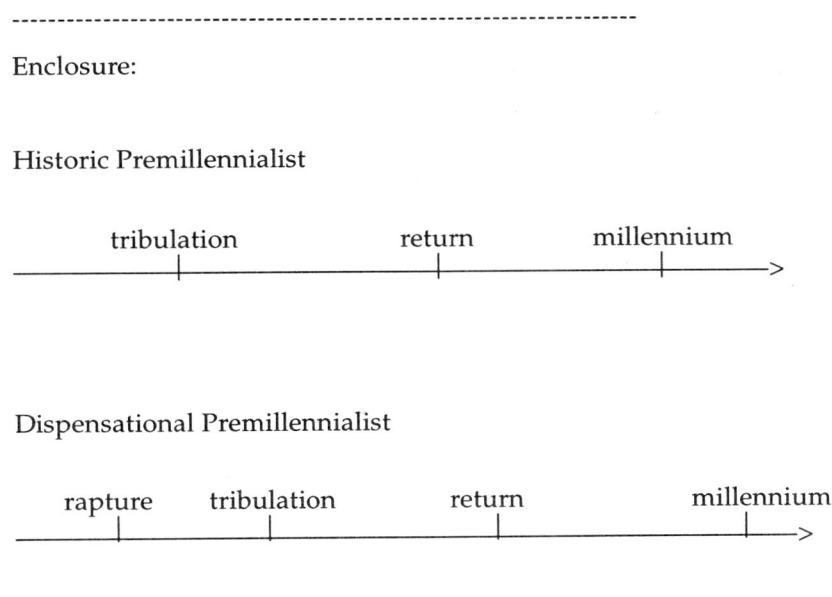

Dispensational Premillennialist

As you can tell, one other difference concerns the tribulation. Most dispensationalists believe Christians will be taken out of history before the tribulation, so they are known as pretribulationists. Most historic premillennialists hold that Christians will go through the tribulation and are posttribulationists.

Some of our church members were familiar with the details of these views, and others felt they were being initiated into a mystery religion! (One of my friends, a retired minister, is going to write a book on "messchatology.") I assured them that the basic issues deserved our best thinking, but they could live long, productive Christian lives without becoming dogmatic on the details.

I concluded my session by saying that there are two basic questions we all need to answer. The questions appear in the story of Hagar in Genesis 16:8. Where have you come from and where are you going? The second question could be answered in some penultimate way (career, marriage), but eschatology reminds us that the questions deserve an ultimate answer. I like to correlate those two questions with Jesus' "answer" in John 16:28 (NIV): "I came from the Father and entered the world; now I am leaving the world and going back to the Father." Without writing a sermon, you can see where I would go with that thought. Christians can answer those questions like Jesus. Ultimately, we come from God and will eventually go to him.

Well, my starting point was that I think detailed discussions of doctrines are better introduced in a teaching context. Since some church members only attend the worship services, however, the main points of any doctrine need to be affirmed there.

We're near the end of our semester here, and I need to write some final exams. It's fitting that the last doctrine I teach each semester is eschatology! Indeed, I tell my students that their grade for the course is like eschatological judgment. Judgment is both a process and a pronouncement. The grade I record at the end of the semester is a public declaration of how well they studied all semester long (the process). At the end, God's judgment should not be a surprise. He will announce what we have determined by our basic decisions all through life.

From: Chris
To: Dr. Mac
Date: May 20
Subject: Millennium—Reply

Just a quick note. Your letter about the millennium inspired me to propose an article to my managing editor. Rather than limit the article to the "isms" of Christian faith, however, I asked her if I could interview representatives of several religions about their views of the end of history. I knew that the approach of the year 2001 had provoked a lot of discussion about the future. She was very receptive to my idea and suggested that I do some preliminary interviews and get back to her with a formal proposal.

12

Keep in Touch

From: Chris
To: Dr. Mac
Date: May 23
Subject: Religion editor

I finally have time to respond more fully to your last e-mail. My life's been pretty hectic lately, kind of like the end of a semester.

Your letter about your presentation on the millennial schemes to the church group brought back a lot of memories of your diagrams on the blackboard. The view you ignored, panmillennialism, was popular with my generation. Everything will work out in the end! Seriously, I may suggest to my pastor that he do a series of classes on eschatology. Maybe he would even invite you to come lead it. I know you do Bible studies in churches, and we're close enough for you to come for a weekend conference.

My biggest news here, however, is about the immediate future, not the end of time. My managing editor has asked me to become the religion editor for our paper. The current religion editor is taking early retirement. He's had some health problems and the company has a very good retirement program. Anyway, the managing editor was very impressed with the occasional articles I had done for the "church" page. My interviews with the pastor who has "visions" and the female pastor and my coverage of the state convention were, she said, "fair and enlightening"! My proposal for an article on the way different religions view the future helped her choose me. I'll get a small raise, and the newspaper will even pay my expenses if I want to take some seminary classes or grad school classes in journalism.

The new position has not helped me resolve my long-range plans. I'm still struggling with whether I should be a "minister" or not. Taking some night classes at the seminary might be the catalyst I need. I know that some of the issues I will need to report as religion editor will demand more theological training than I have.

Our correspondence has really helped me clarify some basic theological issues. I don't feel like I have all the answers, but now I realize that authentic faith does not demand total comprehension and absolute certainty. There always seems to be an element of risk-taking. Thanks for all your help.

P.S. Dr. Mac, I asked Chris to let me add a personal note.

Although we've only met a few times, I understand why
Chris speaks so highly of you. Thanks for taking the time to
write to both of us.
Carolyn

From: Dr. Mac
To: Chris
Date: May 24
Subject: Congratulations!

The news about your new position at the newspaper is
wonderful. Being a religion editor may be a perfect position for you. Your ministerial training and journalistic experience should have prepared you well for your new assignment. You've undoubtedly heard the old statement that
Christians should have a Bible in one hand and a newspaper in the other. In other words, we need to know God's
revelation and the needs of our world. Through your articles you will be able to keep in touch with both. I know
your task will not be to advocate a sectarian position, but
you can enrich the lives of your community by your writing. Religion is a basic aspect of human existence, but it is
often dismissed by the secular media.

I hope you will take some more seminary courses. Whether
or not you consider yourself a "minister" in the professional
or vocational sense, those courses can help you be a better
religion editor. Your editor's offer to finance some semi-

nary courses is rare. A journalist recently wrote: "Major papers and networks encourage reporters to acquire expertise in the law or economics, but I have not heard of any editor asking reporters to brush up their theology." Indeed, an acquaintance, who served as a religion editor for a while, told me that most religion editors have no theological training. I would hope that a finance editor or reporter would have some economics training, so I know some theology, Bible, church history, world religions, and other seminary courses could help you. Indeed, you could be the "theologian-in-residence" for your paper.

I appreciate the kind remarks by you and Carolyn about our correspondence. It's been a joy for me to share in your lives for a while, and I've learned a lot. Keep in touch.

Sources

Page

5   "I like Martin Luther's": Cited in Douglas John Hall, *Thinking the Faith* (Minneapolis, MN: Augsburg, 1989), 237-38.

9   "Your last e-mail reminded me": Douglas John Hall, *Lighten Our Darkness* (Philadelphia, PA: Westminster, 1976), 19.

9   "I still like Tom Skinner's": Tom Skinner, *If Christ Is the Answer, What Are the Questions?* (Grand Rapids, MI: Zondervan, 1974).

9   "To enjoy Theology": University of Oxford, *Undergraduate Prospectus for Entry in 1996-97*, 105.

14   "One textbook in systematic theology": Morris Ashcraft, *Christian Faith and Beliefs* (Nashville, TN: Broadman, 1984), 40-41.

14   "Our textbook from 5 years ago": Millard J. Erickson, *Christian Theology, Volume 1* (Grand Rapids, MI: Baker Book House, 1983).

17   "He would either be a lunatic": C. S. Lewis, *Mere Christianity* (New York, NY: Macmillan, 1943; 1952 reprint) 56.

20   "If you have already looked at Lewis's": Peter Kreeft, *Between Heaven and Hell* (Downers Grove, IL: InterVarsity, 1982).

23   "Robert Short's books on": Robert L. Short, *The Gospel According to Peanuts* (Richmond, VA: John Knox, 1964); *The Parables of Peanuts* (Greenwich, CT: Fawcett Crest, 1968).

27   "One theologian suggested": Dale Moody, *The Word of Truth* (Grand Rapids, MI: Eerdmans, 1981), 421-26.

28   "As one translator": Eugene Peterson, *The Message* (Colorado Springs, CO: NavPress, 1993), 217.

28   "One of my favorite books": D. M. Baillie, *God Was In Christ* (New York, NY: Charles Scribner's Sons, 1948).

35   "Melanchthon's famous dictum": *Melanchthon and Bucer*, Library of Christian Classics 19, ed. Wilhelm Pauck (Philadelphia, PA: Westminster Press, 1969), 21-22.

40   "Outside of the Bible": C. S. Lewis, *The Lion, the Witch and the Wardrobe* (New York, NY: Collier; 1970 reprint).

43   "The idea of God being": J. B. Phillips, *Your God Is Too Small* (New York, NY: Macmillan, 1965), 79-88.

52   "Three of these are": Adapted from Warren McWilliams, "*In Vitro* Fertilization: An Exercise in Biotheology," *Search 21* (Winter 1992): 30.

58   "One theologian proposed": Dorothee Soelle, *Suffering*, trans. Everett R. Kalin (Philadelphia, PA: Fortress, 1975), 73.

59   "If you want to do some reading": C. S. Lewis, *The Problem of Pain* (New York, NY: Macmillan, 1962); Daniel J. Simundson, *Faith Under Fire* (Minneapolis, MN: Augsburg, 1980).

61   "His book": C. S. Lewis, *A Grief Observed* (New York, NY: Bantam, 1976 reprint).

65   "I like the approach": Bradley C. Hanson, *An Introduction to Christian Theology* (Minneapolis, MN: Fortress, 1997), 24-31.

69   "If you want to see": H. Richard Niebuhr, "Theological Unitarianisms," *Theology Today* 60 (July 1983): 150-57.

72   "Several years ago I came across": I. T. Ramsey, "Paradox in Religion," *New Essays on Religious Language*, ed. Dallas M. High (New York, NY: Oxford University Press, 1969), 138-61.

72   "I still use the children's book": Joanne Marxhausen, *3 in 1: A Picture of God* (St. Louis, MO: Concordia, 1973).

84   "A good primer": Gordon D. Fee and Douglas Stuart, *How to Read the Bible for All Its Worth*, second ed. (Grand Rapids, MI: Zondervan, 1983).

88   "As one writer put it": T. B. Maston, *Why Live the Christian Life?* (Nashville, TN: Broadman, 1974), 54.

90   "He proposed *scriptura suprema*": James Leo Garrett, Jr., *Systematic Theology, Volume 1* (Grand Rapids, MI: Eerdmans, 1990), 180.

96   "One of my favorite C. S. Lewis": C. S. Lewis, *The Screwtape Letters* (New York, NY: Macmillan, 1961 reprint).

97   "Incidentally, there is a good book": S. Dennis Ford, *Sins of Omission: A Primer on Moral Indifference* (Minneapolis, MN: Fortress, 1990).

101 "A very interesting book": John W. Cooper, *Body, Soul, and Everlasting Life* (Grand Rapids, MI: Eerdmans, 1989).

105 "Since you graduated": Adapted from William L. Hendricks, *The Doctrine of Man* (Nashville, TN: Convention, 1977), 117.

108 "In my Shakespeare class": *As You Like It*, Act II, Scene 7.

110 "I recently started using": G. R. Osborne, "Tongues, Speaking in," *Evangelical Dictionary of Theology*, ed. Walter A. Elwell (Grand Rapids, MI: Baker Book House, 1984), 1102-3.

113 "Of course, Karl Barth": Karl Barth, *Evangelical Theology: An Introduction*, trans. Grover Foley (Garden City, NY: Anchor Books, 1964), 67.

116 "I used the famous quotation": Henry David Thoreau, *Walden, or, Life in the Woods* (New York, NY: Signet, 1980 reprint), 216.

123 "For me the easiest way": See Dale Moody, *The Word of Truth* (Grand Rapids, MI: Eerdmans, 1981), 308-11.

124 "I also like Paul Tillich's": Paul Tillich, *The Shaking of the Foundations* (New York: Charles Scribner's Sons, 1948), 153-63.

126   "I'm reminded at times of Dietrich Bonhoeffer's": Dietrich
       Bonhoeffer, *The Cost of Discipleship*, trans. Reginald Fuller (New
       York, NY: Macmillan, 1963 reprint), 45-60.

129   "One of my seminary profs, Glenn Hinson": E. Glenn Hinson,
       Seekers After Mature Faith (Waco, TX: Word, 1968).

130   "His book": Richard J. Foster, *Celebration of Discipline* (New
       York, NY: Harper & Row, 1978).

130   "Foster developed this concept": Richard J. Foster, *Freedom of
       Simplicity* (San Francisco, CA: Harper & Row, 1981).

133   "H. Richard Niebuhr's classic": H. Richard Niebuhr, *Christ and
       Culture* (New York, NY: Harper & Row, 1951).

136   "several books by John Howard Yoder": John Howard Yoder,
       The Politics of Jesus (Grand Rapids, MI: Eerdmans, 1972).

136   "Maybe I need to remind them": William Nack, "Does God
       Care Who Wins the Super Bowl?" *Sports Illustrated*, 26 Janu-
       ary 1998, 46-48.

144   "William Willimon's": William H. Willimon, *The Service of
       God* (Nashville, TN: Abingdon, 1983), especially 48-72.

144   "Another writer put it crisply": Theodore W. Jennings, Jr., *Life
       as Worship* (Grand Rapids, MI: Eerdmans, 1982), 10.

144   "One of my favorite illustrations": Soren Kierkegaard, *Purity
       of Heart Is to Will One Thing*, trans. Douglas V. Steere (New
       York, NY: Harper & Row, 1956 reprint), 180-81.

154   "I ordinarily don't want a government": Leon McBeth, "The Ordination of Women," *Review and Expositor* 78 (Fall 1981): 522.

155   "A helpful book by evangelicals": Alvera Mickelsen, ed., *Women, Authority and the Bible* (Downers Grove, IL: InterVarsity, 1986).

156   "Have you seen": Stanley J. Grenz with Denise Muir Kjesbo, *Women in the Church* (Downers Grove, IL: InterVarsity, 1995).

160   "It's": John Claypool, *Tracks of a Fellow Struggler* (Waco, TX: Word, 1974).

161   "When I talked to him after the service": Dale Moody, *The Word of Truth* (Grand Rapids, MI: Eerdmans, 1981), 491-502.

168   "There are only two kinds of people": C. S. Lewis, *The Great Divorce* (New York, NY: Macmillan, 1946).

170   "Several years ago I read": Calvin Miller, *The Philippian Fragment* (Downers Grove, IL: Inter-Varsity, 1982).

180   "A journalist recently wrote": Garry Wills, *Under God: Religion and American Politics* (New York, NY: Simon and Schuster, 1990), 18.